Return of the Tetrad

a novel by

Christopher McIntosh

Published by
Mandrake of Oxford
PO Box 250
OXFORD
OX1 1AP (UK)

A CIP catalogue record for this book is available from the British Library and the US Library of Congress.

978-1-906958-18-3

"The Four Living Creatures, Chariots of Humanity Divine,
Incomprehensible,
In beautiful Paradises expand. These are the Four Rivers of Paradise
And the Four Faces of Humanity, fronting the Four Cardinal Points
Of Heaven, going forward, forward irresistible from Eternity to
Eternity"

William Blake, Jerusalem, Plate 98.

"Take a lie, a myth and a fact and you get somewhere
near the truth."   Sufi saying.

1

The whole thing would never have happened if it hadn't been for the dream, the nightmare. It came again and again, and it was always the same. I was being chased through a forest by a group of men with hounds. I was conscious of being enveloped in a strange costume, made from the skin of some hairy animal. I had on a mask which made breathing difficult. Always at the same point in the dream my flight was arrested by a chasm on the far side of which stood another group of men urging me to jump. I would hesitate, looking fearfully down at the stream that gushed over the rocks far below – hesitate for too long because in another few seconds my pursuers would be upon me and I would fumble the jump. There would be a momentary spinning lunch into the abyss and the up-rushing of jagged rocks. Then I would awake with a cry. I was left with a feeling of terror and of something desperately unresolved.

The dream changed my life because it led me to Gilbert North, and it was thanks to him that I had the extraordinary adventure that I'm going to tell you about. But first you need to know a bit about the kind of person I was before it all happened.

My name is Paul Cairns. By ancestry and upbringing I am Scottish, but I was born in a country village in Buckinghamshire in 1944 while the whirlwind of war still churned its way across half the world. My parents had waited until the tide had turned in the Allies' favour before conceiving me. My earliest memories are of Oxford, where my father, after the leaving the Army Medical Corps, had taken up a teaching post in psychiatry and a fellowship of New College. I remember hushed college quadrangles, hidden gardens with immaculate lawns, the swish of oars on the river, and bells ... endless bells whose mellow tones seemed not to mark the pace of time but rather to slow it down.

The Oxford idyll came to an end when we moved to Edinburgh, where my father had been appointed chief psychiatrist at an Edinburgh hospital for the mentally ill. Despite my Scottish ancestry I found it hard to get used to the Scottish capital – at first it seemed grey and rather gloomy after the mellowness of Oxford. The worst aspect of it was the day school I was sent to at the age of seven or eight. It was run by an elderly man called Pritchard, a scrawny, stooping, shuffling figure with pale, watery eyes and a military moustache. The school was divided into "houses", which Pritchard had named in honour of First World War heroes like General Haig, General Kitchener and Admiral Beatty. I was assigned to the one named after Haig, one of the most criminally incompetent generals in history, as I later found out.

To parents of prospective pupils Pritchard would present an authoritative but avuncular image, a reassuring combination of jollity and old-fashioned firmness. In fact he was a sadist of the worst kind – the kind who finds a moral excuse for his sadism. His favoured instrument of punishment was a leather slipper which he kept in a pile of old newspapers in his study. I must have been about eight or nine years old when I was summoned by him one afternoon – for what offence I had no idea – made to drop my trousers and bend over a chair. When Pritchard hit me with the slipper the pain was so intense that I urinated on the chair. In that moment all my childhood innocence and trust was lost. I became taciturn, emotionally withdrawn and distrustful of the entire adult world. The experience also reinforced an innate touch of masochism in my nature, so that later on the transition to an adult sexual life was extremely difficult for me. Already at that age I was troubled periodically by the recurring nightmare – but more about that later.

Somehow I survived. I developed an arrogant intellectualism as my defence against the world. By the time I went back to Oxford as a student I was an outwardly self-assured but inwardly insecure person who didn't know who he was. I still have a photograph taken of me in the college garden, where I look a bit a character from *Brideshead Revisited* – a slim, callow youth in a white, open-neck shirt, reclining on a lawn reading a book, half my face hidden by a flop of fair hair.

It was around the time that the photograph was taken that I began to be drawn towards mysticism and the occult. One day in the dim and dusty recesses of a second-hand bookshop in Broad Street I spotted a book called *The Doctrine and Ritual of Transcendental Magic* by Eliphas Lévi. Curiosity overcame my rationalist conditioning. I opened the book at random and a passage immediately caught my attention:

"Magic is the traditional science of the secrets of nature which has been transmitted to us from the magi. By means of this science the adept becomes invested with a species of relative omnipotence and can operate super-humanly – that is, after a manner which transcends the normal possibility of man ... To attain the sanctum regnum, in other words, the knowledge and power of the magi, there are four indispensable conditions

– an intelligence illuminated by study, an intrepidity which nothing can check, a will which nothing can break, and a discretion which nothing can corrupt and nothing intoxicate. TO KNOW; TO DARE; TO WILL; TO KEEP SILENCE – such are the four words of the magus ...”

The passage gripped me. It aroused in me a thirst which until that moment I didn't know I had – a thirst for a draught of something stronger and more vital than the coolly rational stuff that I imbibed in the Oxford philosophy syllabus. I bought the book, but having read it I wasn't much the wiser about how to attain the "sanctum regnum" of which Lévi spoke. I went on to read anything I could find on magic, myth and mysticism: Dion Fortune's *Mystical Qabalah*, James Frazer's *Golden Bough*, Robert Graves' *White Goddess*, Margaret Murray's *Witch Cult in Western Europe*. I also became an avid reader of works of occult fiction, like M. R. James's *Ghost Stories of Antiquary* and the creepy tales of H. P. Lovecraft with their hints of ancient dormant forces lying beneath the surface of reality and ready to be called up by objects of special potency. I gained much fascinating, out-of-the-way knowledge, but I saw no way in which I could apply it practice.

One afternoon I had a conversation that I still remember clearly. It was over tea in my lodgings with my friend Peter Rawson. I was just pouring him a cup when he said: "You must meet Gilbert North." And something about the sound of the name gave me a strange sense of premonition.

"Gilbert North," I repeated. I paused with the teapot in my hand, the spout hovering over a cup on the table in front of my chair. The name reached out to me across time. I poured out the cup and handed it to Peter. We had been talking about occultism.

Peter took the cup and settled back into his armchair. "Gilbert North," he went on, "probably knows more about occultism than anyone else in Britain." He took a sip from his cup, slowly rolled and lit a very thin cigarette, then added: "Have you heard of the Order of the Sanctum Regnum?"

"Yes," I said, "wasn't it some sort of esoteric brotherhood that broke up just before the Second World War? And didn't they take the name from Eliphas Lévi?"

Peter nodded. "That's right. The Sanctum Regnum was one of the most effective organizations of its kind in the world. North was a high-grade member of it. After the order broke up, he travelled around India and China studying oriental religions. Then, when his father died, he came back and took over the family estate in Hertfordshire. I've never met anyone quite like him. He lives a sort of double existence: the prosperous country squire on the one hand, the mystic and scholar on the other."

At the moment a double-decker bus came to a halt on the main road outside my ground-floor window, casting a shadow over the contents of the room: the bed in the corner, the heavy, carved sideboard, the disproportionately small wardrobe and the prints and books with which I had made the place my own. The interruption made me conscious of the gathering dusk of the March afternoon, and I drew the curtains and lit the electric fire and the pink-shaded lamp that stood on the mantelpiece.

When I sat down again, Peter was leaning forward in his hunched, bird-like way, scanning the titles in the bookcase that stood to one side of the fireplace. The smoke from his cigarette curled up and made twisting patterns in the lamplight. He turned and looked at me, poking his glasses back into place with a forefinger.

"If you know something about occultism – as I see from your reading that you do – then you would find old North fascinating."

I was flattered that Peter took my interest in the occult seriously, as I held him somewhat in awe. Not only did he look a good ten years older than he was, because of his thin face and prematurely receding hair, but his character seemed focused in a way that is rare in an undergraduate. The impression of age was added to by his donnish way of talking, which was not an affectation. He was obviously marked out for an academic career, and in fact he later became a lecturer in Egyptology.

I asked him how he knew North.

"My tutor introduced me to him," Peter replied, "when I was doing some research on Egyptian ritual magic. North has the most wonderful library which he allowed me to look through. If you like I'll drive you over to his house one day and you can meet him."

Again that feeling of premonition, of a road leading into the mists of an alluring but vaguely disquieting territory. "Yes," I said, "I should very much like to meet the man."

"Right. I'll get in touch with him and see if I can fix a day."

But as it happened Peter never did drive me over to see North. Soon after our conversation the University broke up for the spring vacation, and when we returned for the summer term we quickly found ourselves immersed in work for our final examinations; as these loomed closer other matters were forgotten. After the examinations were over I went off for a long summer holiday and lost touch with Peter. I came back to a job as a junior copy editor in Fleet Street and later landed a job as staff writer on a glossy magazine called the *Townsman*.

Meanwhile I had married Sally. I met her on a train going to London during my last term. I was reading a book when I sensed someone watching me and looked up to see a pair of lively brown eyes, set in a round face with sensual lips, a dainty nose and pale skin set off by a cascade of black hair. We got into conversation. She had sparkle and a kind of wholesome freshness that appealed to me, although at first I didn't imagine her as a potential girl friend – more the type to have a nice warm friendship with. We arranged to meet in London, where she worked for a large travel agency and shared a flat in Putney with three other women. We went to an Indian restaurant where the background music included a strange sitar version of Beethoven's *Für Elise*. Strange how the mind recalls such details. We sat in an alcove lined with green flock wallpaper and something happened. You could say it was love at second sight. Afterwards we went back to her flat and she "sorted me out" as they say, meaning she swept away my sexual hang-ups with a beautiful, passionate intensity that left me totally smitten. Our love affair continued. By the end of the summer she was pregnant and in the autumn we married.

You probably think I'm going to say that marriage was a rude awakening, but it wasn't. We settled down happily in a flat in West

Hampstead, then moved to the commuter town of Gorehamstead in Hertfordshire when our son Mark was one year old. It's remarkable how life changes as soon as you have a family. Suddenly you're thinking about things like school catchment areas and house prices and the best neighbourhoods in which to bring up children. I became so immersed in the role of family man and breadwinner that for a while my occult interests were pushed into the background. That would all change when I met Gilbert North, but first I must explain what led up to the meeting.

2

One weekend in early spring a couple we knew were staying in the house as our guests. On Saturday afternoon I suggested a drive to Stowmead, a picturesque village near by that we had never visited. The journey was rewarded as the village was an unusually beautiful one, situated in a hollow and clustered round a green with a duck pond. At one side of the pond was an old stocks and whipping-post. I wondered whether the inhabitants of the pretty half-timbered houses by the green had enjoyed seeing the plight of the poor wretches who were punished there or whether perhaps they had kept away from their windows at such times, the way we turn the page when we see a newspaper photograph of an atrocity.

We parked the car at the side of the green and took a path that led out of the village and up a hill through some mature beech woods. At the top the trees cleared, and we had a fine view in all directions. Away to the west, far beyond the woods through which we had climbed, a tiny train moved silently northward along a shallow valley. To the east there were more beech woods, stretching their incomparable green toward the distant towers of some great house.

We returned to the village by the same path and noticed a sign announcing that one of the half-timbered cottages served teas. Our thoughts turned toward buttered scones and farm eggs, and we were soon seated in a low-ceilinged room, with four tables and a huge carved oak sideboard that filled half of one wall, being served a tea that fully lived up to our expectations. From our table by the window we could see the church. It lay just a little distance from the main part of the village, and we had not noticed it when we arrived. After tea we walked over to have a look at it.

The church was solidly built with a square tower, and the walls were faced with the flint that abounds in that part of Hertfordshire. From the outside it was a trifle clumsy, but inside the proportions were lovely, and the solid stonework and rough-hewn carvings were medieval. Hatchments and sepulchral monuments could be glimpsed in the gloom against the walls of the nave, and a faintly musty but not unpleasant smell pervaded the place. At the western end of the church was a carved stone font, and I had stopped to admire this when I heard my five-year-old son call from another part of the building.

"What is it, Mark?" I said.

"Come and see this, Daddy," he called excitedly.

I went to where he was standing, in a small chamber to the south, divided off from the rest of the nave by a carved stone screen. In the middle of the chamber was a tomb on which reposed the stone effigies of a man and woman. The man was clad in armour, and both he and his lady had their hands in the position of prayer.

"Look," said Mark, "What's that?" He was pointing at a creature on which the feet of the man rested. I had often seen dogs or other animals supporting the feet of the tomb effigies, but this figure was like nothing I had ever come across before, on a tomb or anywhere else. It was a small figure, human in shape, but covered from head to toe in thick hair. Around the waist was a belt of vine leaves. The creature was reclining propped up on one hand. The other hand held a club shaped like a tree trunk with lopped-off branches.

I stood staring at the object, and as I did so a dizziness came over me. It was as though the little carved figure had touched off some reflex lying deep within me. It produced in me a feeling akin to that caused by the discovery of some childhood memento which had lain forgotten in a bottom drawer. And yet the analogy is not quite accurate, for it did not immediately bring any images or memories to my mind – only a vague but powerful feeling of disquiet. The figure had some association for me, I was sure of that, but for a minute or so I could not put my finger on it. Then all at once the figure came to life in my mind. It moved, it ran, and I ran with it, keeping pace like a shadow. And then it was as though I became the shadow of all the hunted things in the world – of the stag as it starts across the hillside at the sniff of an alien scent on the wind, of the fox as it hears the baying of hounds and the sound of the horn, of the escaped prisoner fleeing across a bleak moor and hearing the sound of helicopters overhead. And then I suddenly knew that I had awoken many times with the same feeling – and always after the same dream. That was the answer: in some strange way the little stone carving was linked with my recurring nightmare.

I emerged from a semi-trance to find myself looking at a printed notice fixed to the wall. It explained that the tomb figures were those of Sir Robert Whitworth, Bt., and his wife, Mary. Sir Robert had been a local landowner and had been killed at the battle of Tewksbury in 1471 during the Wars of the Roses. His body had been brought back to the church at Stowmead, and the tomb had lain there ever since. No trace of the family existed today.

I must have been unusually silent on the journey home, for when Sally and I were alone that evening she asked me if anything was the matter. I was still too confused in my own mind to be able to talk coherently about what was troubling me, so I told her that I was only feeling tired. I hoped that by the morning my feeling of uneasiness would have passed, but I went to bed half afraid that the dream would occur again. As it happened I slept perfectly well and dreamlessly. When I awoke my feeling of disquiet had passed, but in its place was a determination to find out the connection – if there was one – between my dream and the little man on the tomb.

It seemed to me that the first step was to find out as much as I could about the history and symbolic significance of the figure. I set about my researches as soon as I returned to work on Monday morning. In the magazine's reference library were a number of books on heraldry, and I began by searching through these. The first thing I discovered was that the figure was known as a "wild man" or "woodwose" and that it was one of the traditional heraldic motifs. In England it was comparatively rare, but in Scottish and continental heraldry it was more common. Usually the wild man stood as a supporter at the side of the shield in a set of armorial bearings, often opposite his female counterpart. More rarely the figure appeared as a charge on the shield itself. I remained unenlightened about the origin of the symbol. Nor could I find any reference to the arms of the Whitworth family. I therefore decided to consult the College of Arms. I telephoned the College and was told that one of the heralds would see me the following morning at twelve o'clock.

A light drizzle was falling on the gloomy commercial buildings of Queen Victoria Street as I walked up from Blackfriars tube station the next day, with the Thames a cold, clammy presence near at hand. The City was at its most grey and forbidding, but once I was past the ornate gates of the College of Arms the gloom took on a grace and elegance that found its expression in soft red brick, dark wooden panelling and the occasional burst of heraldic panoply over a doorway. I announced myself to an ancient porter and a few minutes later found myself entering a room that was less like an office than the study of a country house. A bracket clock over a fine stone mantelpiece chimed twelve as I went in, and an imposing, grey-haired man rose from behind a large mahogany desk and shook my hand, then waved me to a chair opposite him. He had the plump, pink face and benevolent expression of a country clergyman, and when he spoke it was as though to a visitor seeking recondite information from the parish archives.

"Well now," he began, peering at me over the top of his glasses, "you were the chap who wanted to know about the arms of Whitworth."

I nodded.

"I looked up one or two books before you came," he went on, "but all I found was this." He opened a large, leather-bound book containing lists of armorial bearings and showed me the entry for Whitworth. It confirmed what I had thought: the shield was supported by two wild men.

"The title," he explained, "fell into abeyance in the 16th century, and I am afraid very little is known about the family."

"I didn't expect to find out a great deal," I replied, "but the wild man is a well known motif is it not? I wondered if you might be able to tell me how it came into being."

The herald closed the book and placed it on a shelf behind him before replying. "It's not as easy to answer that as you might think. Heraldic motifs do not always readily yield their origins. It's rarely possible to give a cut-and-dried explanation for some particular figure or device. In this case..." He paused and tilted his head to one side. "There are a number of possible explanations for the origin of the symbol. At jousting competitions there used to be a kind of fancy-dress parade, and one of the standard costumes was that of a wild man. The knights who went to the joust would be on the look-out for devices to put on their shields, and the wild man would be an obvious choice. It is also known that noblemen with names like Wood or Forest incorporated the device in their arms as a kind of play on the name."

"But surely," I interrupted, "it must go deeper than that. The figure itself must have had some symbolic meaning to the noblemen who used it."

The herald tapped a silver paper knife on the desk and gave me a slightly evasive look. "I doubt it," he said. "You must remember that the original purpose of all heraldic designs was simply to distinguish one nobleman from another in battle or in the joust when they were covered in armor."

There was an awkward silence. I had the impression that he knew more than he had told me. There was some important piece of information that he was holding back. But why?

"Of course you could be right," he went on. "There might be some ancient legend behind the wild man figure, but that's really the province of the folklorist and not the student of heraldry."

There seemed to be little point in prolonging the interview, so I rose to my feet and thanked him for his trouble.

"Not at all," he said genially, walking with me to the door. "I'm sorry I was not able to be of more help."

I left the College of Arms wondering what clue I could follow up next. "The province of the folklorist," he had said. Very well, I would study the folklore of the wild man. The following day I called on a well-known library specializing in folklore and related subjects, but it contained only one book that even mentioned the wild man, and then only as a passing reference. The elderly lady who ran the library was polite but unable to help.

By then my obsession with the subject had lessened, and over the next few weeks I gradually forgot all about it. Then something happened that brought the issue to my mind again. One morning I awoke in the early hours to find that Sally had switched on the light and was leaning over me.

"What is it, Paul? What's the matter, Darling?" she was saying.

I turned and looked at her, puzzled.

"You were shouting just now at the top of your voice," she told me.

Then I remembered. "It was that dream again," I said.

"The one you have every few months?"

I nodded.

"Don't you think you ought to do something about it?" she said. "See a doctor perhaps."

"I don't know. Perhaps I will if it goes on."

I was worried, for this time the dream had been more vivid than before. I took me some time to go back to sleep, and when I awoke it was with the determination to resume my quest –though what my next move was to be I had no idea. I pondered over the problem for several days, then the following weekend I had a stroke of luck. I had spent Saturday morning doing some overtime work at the office and after lunching at a pub in the Strand I decided to go to Jenkins' bookshop off the Charing Cross Road for a browse.

Anyone with a serious bent for occult or mystical literature sooner or later finds his way to Jenkins' doorway. And once he has found his way there it is more than likely that the shop will become a second home; for the place has a magnetism that is hard to describe to someone who has never been enticed in there by the faint odour of incense that always fills the air, or by the promise of hidden knowledge and strange new pathways. It is more than just a bookshop. It is a meeting place, a club and for many almost a school. I have known similar shops in Paris and New York and San Francisco, but none with quite the same magic as Jenkins'. I have said that the shop catered for student of mysticism or occultism, but that gives rather too narrow an impression of the range of books and of the clientele, for you will also find there the vegetarian dietician and the flying saucer enthusiast. The shop is divided into two sections, which were once separate premises but now have a connecting door between them. One half houses books on ritual magic, divination and similar subjects, while the other is devoted to more sober areas such as oriental religions and Christian mysticism. The former part is usually the more crowded.

The proprietor, Arthur Jenkins, was a small, benign-looking, grey-haired man who had been running the shop for more than forty years and knew the world of occultism like the back of his hand. He was a wise and kind man who, in spite of having lived his life among books, saw his fellow men with a humane and un-bookish eye. Many a lost soul had wandered into the shop, been quietly diagnosed by Jenkins and sent away with the one book on the shelves that could change his life. I had been going to the shop from time to time ever since my Oxford days, and I had a nodding acquaintance with Jenkins. Now, as

I entered the place, it suddenly occurred to me that he might be able to solve my problem. In fact, I felt silly not to have thought of it before. It seemed likely that with his wide knowledge of out-of-the-way subjects he might at least be able to put me on the right trail.

He listened politely to my question then rubbed his chin thoughtfully. "That's a tricky one," he said. "I know of no book that would give you more than a sketchy reference. But wait a bit, there's a chap in the shop now who may be able to help you. Hold on a minute." He disappeared into the part of the shop that drew the crowds and returned a few seconds later shaking his head. "No, I'm sorry, you just missed him. He left the shop only a few minutes ago. But you might still catch him this afternoon. He told my assistant that he is going to an occult conference at the Greenmantle Hotel in Bloomsbury, so why not go along? It's a quarter to two now, and the conference starts at half past, so you should have plenty of time."

"What does he look like?" I asked, feeling a little doubtful about approaching a stranger and asking for help with my rather bizarre problem.

"Oh, you'll recognize him easily," Jenkins assured me. "He's a tall man in his late sixties with an aquiline sort of face. He wears glasses and usually smokes a pipe. His name is North, by the way, Gilbert North."

For some reason it was not until after I had telephoned Sally to tell her my plans and walked half way to Bloomsbury that the name rang a bell. Then suddenly I remembered that afternoon in Oxford and Peter Rawson telling me about a man I should meet who had been a high-ranking member of a magical order and who knew more about occultism than anyone else in Britain. Now at last after five years I had an opportunity to meet him. With a mounting feeling of excitement I quickened my pace toward Bloomsbury.

The hotel was in Great Russell Street, not far from the British Museum, and was a large Edwardian building which had been rather clumsily "modernized" inside. When I enquired about the conference I was directed to a large room in the basement that looked as though it was much used for businessmen's conferences. At one end a blackboard and a table with microphones and decanters of water stood ready for the speakers. I bought a ticket from a young woman at the door and made my way to a seat in the middle of the room. The programme told me that there were to be four lectures, on Kabbalism, witchcraft, Celtic mysticism and something called the Enochian system. I had hoped that Gilbert North might be among the speakers, but he was not.

As I waited for the proceedings to start the room began to fill up with a varied collection of people who took their seats or stood about chatting. Some were totally conventional looking, others eccentric in the extreme. Among the latter were a hatchet-faced man of about forty dressed in a Norfolk jacket with long grey hair swept into a bun at the back of his head, and two people whom I took to be witches – a woman with a bright crimson hooded robe carrying a jewelled sword, and a young man in a similar, but black, robe holding a sceptre. There was also a man dressed in a conventional expensive-looking tweed suit, but who had a most arresting appearance. He had a square face which in colour was almost as white as his hair. His eyes, however, were large and dark, giving the appearance of a pair of coals dropped on a patch of snow. I wondered for a moment whether he might be North, but he did not answer to the description that Jenkins had given me.

My scrutiny of the audience was interrupted by the tapping of a gavel, and I glanced up to see that it was being wielded by a young woman who looked as though she might be more at home on a hockey field than in a gathering such as this. She was unpretentiously dressed and her pink, rather square face had no trace of make-up.

"Ladies and gentlemen," she began, "before we start I should like to say how nice it is to see so many of you here today, especially as some of our speakers have very kindly come from distant parts of the country to give us the benefits of their knowledge. We have tried as in past years, to select a wide variety of subjects, and we hope that you will all find something to interest you in this afternoon's talks. And now it gives me great pleasure to introduce our first speaker, Ivor Llewellyn, whose reputation as a Kabbalist is, I am sure, already known to many of you. Mr. Llewellyn is going to talk to us on the very original-sounding theme of 'The Arthurian Kabbalah'. Mr. Llewellyn."

The speaker was a short, rather plump, neatly dressed man with a pink face and a jovial manner. "In case," he began, "some of you are not familiar with the Kabbalah I am going to explain briefly what it is all about. But bear with me for moment while I prepare some visual aids." He turned and began to draw on the blackboard with a piece of white chalk.

My interest was aroused. I had read Dion Fortune's book and a few other things on the Kabbalah and found it intriguing. I knew that it was a Jewish mystical tradition which had been widely adapted by non-Jewish thinkers, and that it featured a diagram of the basic forces of the universe called the Tree of Life. The thing consisted of ten circles connected by lines and arranged vertically in three triangles with an odd circle at the bottom.

"This," he announced, standing back and pointing at the drawing, "is a cosmic hat stand. Everything in the universe hangs on ten pegs. Galaxies, human beings, micro-organisms, societies, civilizations, plants – all of these are merely different collections of hats hanging on the same ten basic pegs. The ancient Hebrews knew this and gave names and a structure to these ten pegs which reflected their universal character. They are called *Sephiroth*, and their names are: Kether, Chockmah, Binah, Chesed, Geburah, Tiphereth, Netzach, Hod, Jesod, Malkuth; or, in English: the Crown, Wisdom, Understanding, Mercy, Severity, Beauty, Victory, Splendour, the Foundation, the Kingdom."

I was beginning to like the speaker's approach to the subject, and for the time being I forgot my purpose in coming to the meeting. Llewellyn went on to explain that the Sephiroth formed a good basis for meditational exercises, since if one could understand them one would understand the universe itself. One could, for instance, begin at the bottom of the tree and work one's way up to the topmost point where one could attain a vision of the absolute. He said that the Hebrew nature of the system often made it appear alien to the British people and that he had attempted to relate it to our own Arthurian tradition. The Tree of Life became King Arthur's castle, with a central staircase and branching corridors leading to various chambers corresponding to points on the Tree, each of which was characterized by a motif from the Arthurian legends. By working one's way upwards in the imagination one reached the watchtower at the top and gained a view over the magical land of Logres.

After he had finished talking various people asked him questions. One of them came from a man sitting in the front row who asked what ritual the speaker would consider an appropriate means of setting the tone for the meditation. Llewellyn replied that a ritual was not really necessary, but that the ritual of the pentagram could be used if the meditator wished.

"And what correspondence," asked the questioner, "would you give to the false eleventh *Sephira*?"

"You mean Daath?" said Llewellyn.

"Precisely. The hidden sphere that floats in the abyss below the supernal trinity."

The speaker was slightly disconcerted. "There has always been some doubt," he said, "about the true place of Daath in the Kabbalistic tradition. I believe that the system I have outlined is more meaningful if we stick just to the ten true *Sephiroth*."

The questioner did not seem satisfied. "But in that case your castle is dead – a mere structure of stones and mortar."

At this point the chair intervened. "It's a debatable point," she said, "which perhaps would be a good topic of conversation for the tea interval, but before that we have another speaker whom I should now like to introduce. Morag McEwan is going to talk to us about Celtic seasonal festivals."

Ivor Llewellyn stepped down and a small, stocky woman with untidy grey hair, dressed in tweeds, took his place and began to speak in a Scottish accent. But I found it difficult to listen. Some words used by the questioner had, for some reason, stuck in my mind: "the hidden sphere that floats in the abyss..." Since I knew little of the Kabbalah the phrase was almost gibberish to me, but it seemed to hold some special power and kept repeating itself, mantra-like, in my mind. At the same time I watched the back of the questioner's head. I could not be sure, but I had guessed from the authoritative tone of his voice who he might be. Then he turned to speak to someone behind him, and I knew at once that he was Gilbert North. I had a momentary glimpse of a powerful profile like the Duke of Wellington's – an aquiline nose, a strong chin and a tall forehead. I absorbed little of Morag McEwan's speech and waited impatiently for the tea interval when I hoped to introduce myself to North. But I was out of luck. As soon as the interval was announced I was seized upon by the man sitting next to me who asked what I had thought of the speeches. He was an old man with a face like a lizard. Barely had he heard my reply before he launched into an exposition of his theory of life, matter, and the cosmos. He pursued me to the tea counter gabbling of Ancient Wisdom, Yin and Yang, flying saucers. I had already noticed with dismay that North was deep in conversation with Llewellyn, no doubt continuing their discussion on Daath. In any case there was by now no hope of escape. My determined companion continued his monologue until tea was over. He was silenced only by the chair's announcement that we were about to be addressed on the Enochian system. This and the talk on witchcraft that followed were interesting and held my attention, but after the meeting was over I hurried over to the door to catch North.

I struggled through the crowd and reached the front entrance of the hotel just in time to see North disappearing into the twilight of Great Russell Street. He was half way to the corner of Tottenham Court Road before I caught up with him.

"Mr. North?" I panted as I came abreast of him.

"Yes." He turned with a slight start and slowed his pace.

"My name is Paul Cairns. I meant to try to talk to you at the conference, but I didn't get a chance. Mr. Jenkins of the bookshop recommended that I get in touch with you."

He smiled and extended his hand. "How do you do. Old Jenkins put you on to me did he? I expect you want to interrogate me for some newspaper or other."

"No," I said. "It was something rather different. My enquiry has to do with wild men."

North stopped in his tracks and looked at me for a moment before walking on. "Wild men? Good God, why on Earth are you interested in them?"

I was struck by the way he said "them". It was as though he were referring to something vaguely sinister.

"It's long story," I explained and told him as briefly as I could about the dream and the wild man in Stowmead church. By the time I had finished we were standing at the corner of Tottenham Court Road and North was looking at me intently, his glasses glinting from the street lights.

"Dear me," he said. "These are deep waters. Deep and rather treacherous. You'd better come and see me at my house. Then we can have a proper talk. How about lunch next Saturday?"

I accepted eagerly. His home, he told me, was a house called Ravenhurst, which happened to be only ten miles from where I lived. After he had given me directions he hailed a taxi.

"Can I give you a lift anywhere?" he asked. "I'm heading for my flat near the Bayswater Road."

I shook my head and explained that I was going to Euston station, reflecting that North must be a man of substance to be able to afford a country house and a London flat.

"Goodbye then," he said. "I'll look forward to seeing you next Saturday."

Before the lights went out in the back compartment of the taxi I saw him light a huge pipe. Then the windows went dark and the taxi swept away and turned down a side street heading west. I walked up Tottenham Court Road and along Euston Road. A full moon was shining. "The sphere that floats in the abyss..."

3

By the following Saturday spring had taken hold. It was a splendid day and I sang to myself as I drove through the countryside to keep my appointment with North. Earlier in the week I had looked up

Ravenhurst in a book on the country homes of England and had learned that it had been built in the Middle Ages as a country retreat for the abbots of St. Albans and had been used as such until the Reformation when it had been presented to one Simon North who had performed some service for Henry VIII. The North family later became impoverished and were forced to sell the house, but one of them prospered again during the Industrial Revolution and bought it back. The family had held it since then.

I found the village of Coombe Raven which had some Georgian alms-houses, a pleasant-looking pub, and a modern housing estate. Half a mile further on a pair of gateposts topped by stone ravens marked the entrance to North's domain. From there the driveway wound past rhododendron bushes and across a stream by a stone balustraded bridge. Half a mile from the gates I came in sight of the house. From its description I had been prepared for something imposing and perhaps rather forbidding. But the house that came into view at the end of a fine avenue of chestnut trees was altogether more friendly-looking than I had expected. It was a mixture of many different periods. A half-timbered Tudor section stood cheek-by-jowl with an elegant 18th-century stone facade, which in turn was flanked by a later brick accretion, and poking out from the middle of the jumble what appeared to be the gable of a medieval chapel.

The drive led through another gateway and into a walled courtyard. The car crunched to a halt on the gravel, and as I stepped out a large black labrador padded up to me with tail wagging and gave me a friendly nudge. A few seconds later my host emerged from the porticoed front door dressed in an old faded sports jacket, flannel trousers, and a pair of brown brogues. He extended his right hand and with his left removed the enormous pipe from his teeth.

"Find your way here all right?" he asked, shaking my hand. "Good. Come inside." And he ushered me through the front door, up a small flight of steps and into a magnificent great hall whose walls soared upward to a majestic oak-beamed roof. North explained that it had been the abbot's banqueting hall.

It was a house full of surprises. We mounted a Victorian panelled stairway, crossed through a small room which was all that remained of the chapel, and descended by another stair to a stone-flagged dining hall with a large oak refectory table. Two doors led off this room. One opened into a big drawing room with chintz-covered furniture and family portraits, the other led to North's study, another big room with white-painted woodwork and the walls lined from floor to ceiling with books. On a round mahogany table in the middle stood a bronze effigy of a Buddha. A vast desk strewn with pipes and papers occupied the bay window commanding a superb view over a stretch of lawn sloping down to an orchard.

"Let's have some sherry, shall we?" North invited and waved me to one of the old leather-covered armchairs by the fireplace and began to rummage in a cupboard for glasses. As he poured the sherry I noticed the ring on his left hand – a heavy gold ring with a heraldic engraving on it. Noticing the direction of my gaze, he took off the ring and handed it to me. The engraving showed a heraldic shield divided into quarters, in which were the symbols of the four alchemical elements.

They were indicated by triangles, upright and reversed for fire and water, and again upright and reversed with a line through the middle for air and earth.

"The elements," he said, slipping the ring back on to his finger, are one manifestation of a universal tetrad – a fourfold pattern – which we shall speak more about another time."

He handed me a glass of sherry, and as I sipped it I noticed a little unframed photograph propped up on the mantlepiece. It showed a big, powerful-looking man with strangely staring eyes seen in bright sunlight in what appeared to be a North African setting. He was seated on some kind of rampart with minarets rising in the distance behind him. Though his features were European he was dressed in burnous and turban.

"He looks a bit fierce, doesn't he?" said North, reading my thoughts as he handed me a glass of sherry. "But he rather enjoyed being thought of like that."

"Who is he?" I asked.

"Nicholas Hadley. You've heard of him?"

North could see from my reaction that I had. I remembered that Hadley had once been head of the order of the Sanctum Regnum and had acquired a public reputation as a black magician of the darkest hue. When I timidly asked if there was any foundation to his notoriety my host waved his hand impatiently.

"Look here," he said, sitting down and lighting his pipe, "'Black magic' is a term used by simpletons for things they are afraid of or don't understand or both. To talk about 'black magic' is like talking about 'black electricity'. Magic is like any other force – it can be used for good or evil purposes. But it differs from other forces in that when it is used for evil, that evil always in the end rebounds on the person who is so using it. This means that anyone who consciously practices so-called 'black magic' is either a foolish dilettante – and there are quite a few of those – or else someone so committed to evil that he is willing to sacrifice himself to the powers of darkness, in other words a veritable saint of evil – and of these there are very few." He paused and tossed a match into the empty grate of the fire. "You see," he went on, "the true saint of evil must perform miracles of darkness as the saint of good must perform miracles of light."

He sat for a few moments and stared silently into the empty fireplace, puffing strongly at his pipe. Now that I was sitting face to face with him I had begun to notice things that had escaped my attention before. His eyes had a slightly hooded appearance and his teeth had a suggestion of wolfish fangs. He frequently punctuated his remarks with a kind of suppressed laugh – a series of rapid puffs of breath. I make him sound sinister, but he was not so in the least, for his face had a noble cast, and his eyes beneath their hoods were full of humour and compassion.

I was eager to get him to expand on the subject of magic. "These saints of evil that you speak of – have you ever known any?" I asked.

"One," he replied "and then only indirectly. I never met him face to face, but I saw some of the things that he could do – and I don't want to see them again if I can help it."

"Do you know his name?"

"No, not even that. No one I know has ever met him – they have only seen his underlings. Hadley and I used to call him 'L.O.Q.', the Lord of the Qliphoth." And by way of explanation he added that in the Kabbalistic tradition the Qliphoth were the realms of unbalanced force in the universe, inhabited by all manner of unpleasant entities. "I can tell you this, though..." he continued, bending forward to tap the ashes from his pipe into the grate. "All his life he has been searching for a thing that will increase his evil power a thousandfold. I have that thing, and as long as I have it his power will be limited." As he said this he looked me directly in the eyes, then added: "What I have just told you must not go beyond these four walls."

I nodded. "May I ask what it is?"

"It's called the Talisman of Althotas," North replied without hesitation. "I can't show it to you because it's locked away behind protective barriers – magical barriers – and to break the seals is a complex operation."

There was not a trace of the melodramatic in the way he told me these things. A psychiatrist would doubtless have concluded that he suffered from some complex form of paranoia, but I accepted implicitly the truth of what he said, even though I am not given to credulity. He sensed my acceptance and went on talking.

"The talisman," he said, "is a perfect example of a magical tool that can be used for good or ill. It has a long history. No one knows exactly where or when it was made, but it is first recorded in the possession of the Sicilian magus Cagliostro. He became over-ambitious and tried to use it to bring himself wealth, and he died in a prison of the Holy Inquisition. It then passed into the hands of an evil French adept who used it to bring about the Reign of Terror in 1792, but he perished on the guillotine. After that there is no record of it until it crops up in the possession of another French magician, Eliphas Lévi. He used it only for good purposes, and he cured many sick people with its power. When Lévi died in 1875 he bequeathed it to an English occultist who was Hadley's teacher and gave it to Hadley before he died. Hadley in turn passed it on to me and warned me that L.O.Q. would do his utmost to get his hands on it."

"Does he know you have it?" I asked.

"I think not, because no one has yet attempted to steal it. But it could be that no one dared to do so, knowing of the efficacy of the barriers."

"What would happen if anyone tried to break through them?"

North smiled grimly. "He would be blasted by the forces that I have bound to guard the talisman. It would be as though several thousand volts had passed through his body."

I was not inclined to disbelieve him and shuddered slightly at the thought of such an effective magical burglar defense. I was just beginning to wonder whether it could be used against ordinary burglars when a gong sounded in the next room.

"Ah, that will be lunch," said North, standing up. "Shall we go in? We shall be on our own. My wife is staying in Washington with our elder son. He works in the British embassy there."

We sat down corner to corner at one end of the large refectory table, and lunch was served by a plump, fresh-faced girl who looked perhaps eighteen or nineteen. "Local girl," North explained. "My wife taught her how to cook."

"Your wife must be a good teacher," I commented, savouring the game casserole that the maid had cooked.

"Are you married?" he asked me.

I replied that I was, and he went on to ask me a series of questions about myself: where I was born, who my parents were, where I was educated. I began to wonder when we were going to discuss my problem, but it was not until the meal was over that he raised the topic.

We had moved to a little paved area by some French windows at the edge of the garden, and sat there in silence for a few minutes, sipping coffee while butterflies hovered in the sunshine over some foxgloves in the flowerbed near us.

"Well now," said my host, breaking the silence, "about this dream of yours. How long have you been having it?"

I told him that I had had it for as long as I could remember.

"I see. And when you saw the figure on the tomb at Stowmead you connected it with the dream?"

"Yes."

"Tell me exactly what you felt when you saw the figure." As I did so North nodded occasionally as though what I was saying confirmed his thoughts. When he had finished he sat silently puffing at his pipe, evidently deep in thought.

"What do you think is the explanation?" I said at last.

Instead of answering he asked: "Have you ever read any of the literature on dreams?"

"A little," I replied.

"Then you are probably aware of all the traditional theories about dreams, and perhaps also some of the less orthodox ones – such as reincarnation theory."

"Yes," I said with some reservation in my voice. "I know that some people believe that some dreams are memories of past lives."

"But I can tell that you are sceptical. Let's take a walk around the garden and I'll see if I can change your mind."

The garden, like the house, was full of surprises. High hedges and old stone walls divided off lawn from rose garden, and orchard from kitchen garden, and one unexpected secret corner from the next.

"The point is," said North as we walked across a lawn toward the orchard, "that the psychologists would have their own explanation for your dream, based on their own assumptions. They would probably dig out all manner of complexes and sexual problems. But they would be barking up the wrong tree, for I can see from what you have told me about yourself that you are basically a well-balanced person. No, your average psychiatrist would miss the all-important fact. Your dream, I believe, is not symbolic; it is a memory of an event that actually happened, and happened before you were born."

"Do you mean to say," I asked feeling a little incredulous, "that in a previous incarnation I was chased over the edge of a cliff and killed?"

"Exactly," said North.

"But for what reason?"

"I have a theory about that, but I would rather not tell you what it is until I have tested it. And to do that will require some simple hypnosis. Are you willing to submit yourself to that?"

I had reservations about hypnosis, but my instinctive trust for North overcame them, and I agreed.

"Good," he said. "Let's go back to my study."

When he had once again seated me before his fireplace he took out a small tape-recorder and placed it on a table beside me. "This is to record what you say during hypnosis," he explained. "Sometimes it's useful later to have an exact record." Then he produced a candle, lit it and placed it in a holder up on the mantlepiece. Finally he drew the curtains, and the room was ready.

Standing in front of me and slightly to the side, he told me to look at the candle without tilting my head back, so that it was a slight strain to keep my eyes on the flame. Of what happened next I have only the haziest recollection. He began to talk in a quiet, slow, rhythmical way, telling me to keep my gaze fixed on the candle. Then there was some counting, and the next thing I knew I was wide awake and he was switching off the tape recorder.

"It's just as I thought," he said, drawing back the curtains. "Under hypnosis you recounted the whole episode."

The light that came into the room from outside was dull, and looking at my watch I was astonished to see that it was half past five.

"Have I really been under all that time?" I asked.

"Yes," he said. "You must be ready for some tea." And he opened the door and called some instructions to the maid. A few minutes later a tray arrived. North handed me a cup of tea and some buttered toast, both of which I consumed as though I had just climbed a mountain.

"I can now explain," he said, "the exact significance of your dream – your experience perhaps I should say. What do you know about the figure of the wild man?"

I shrugged. "All I know is that it is a medieval motif often found in churches and on tombs."

"Correct, but it is more than just a motif. It was the sign of a medieval secret fraternity, the Brotherhood of the Wild Men. The fact that the figure appears on the tomb of your Sir Robert Whitworth shows that he was a member of the brotherhood."

"And what sort of brotherhood was it?" I asked.

He refilled the cups and sat down before replying. "The purpose of it was the same as that of most occult societies, namely to develop the members' higher nature and thereby endow them with powers to do good. The name is deliberately misleading, for the wild man figure represents the lower, animal nature of man which had to be transcended. The members went through a number of grades of initiation corresponding to the spheres of the Kabbalistic Tree of Life. There was an outer order composed of those who had passed through the first seven grades and a very small inner order for those who had crossed the abyss by discovering the secret, hidden sphere of Daath, the ultimate link between the supernal trinity and the lower seven spheres."

Suddenly I remembered the lecture at the Bloomsbury hotel. "That's what you meant when you talked about the 'sphere that floats in the abyss'."

He nodded, "All higher religious systems have a similar concept in their mystical traditions. When your consciousness reaches that point you can look two ways. Up toward God or down toward man."

"And where do I come in?" I asked.

"You," he said, "Many centuries ago were a member of the brotherhood and a candidate for admission to the inner order. The experience that you have been re-living in your dreams was the ordeal of initiation. You failed that ordeal, and the memory of the failure has lived with you ever since. Now you are faced with two choices. You can either reconcile yourself to remaining outside the brotherhood, or you can take the test again."

"You mean the brotherhood still exists?"

"In a sense, yes. Brotherhoods come and go, but the spirits behind them remain on the inner planes. You see there are really only two brotherhoods. One worships light and the other darkness. If you want to seek admission to the brotherhood of light then you must take the test that you failed in your previous life, but it will not be taken on this plane. Your examiners will be the Secret Chiefs of the Inner Planes."

"What will the test be?" I asked.

"Probably a reconstruction on the Inner Plane of the one you took before. But I should warn you that the perils of failure are infinitely greater than they were before. It could mean total destruction of your soul, so that instead of being reborn into another life you are cast into the abyss and annihilated. And don't forget that on the Inner Planes there are evil entities waiting to trip you up at every turn – entities whose power on the physical plane would be limited."

"And what if I decide not to take the test?"

North shrugged. "You will have peace of mind – I can see to that. But you will make no further progress in this lifetime or even probably in the next. You will have a long, hard climb over many more incarnations before your soul is given the same chance again."

I hesitated, thinking of North's alarming words – total destruction of the soul, annihilation in the abyss. Yet a voice in me said that it would be cowardly to turn back now.

"I need to think about it," I said.

"Of course. Give me a call when you have made a decision. If you do decide to go ahead it would be advisable for you to stay the night here."

* * *

By the time I returned home I had made up my mind to take North's test, but I toned it down for Sally, merely telling her that I thought he could help with the problem of the dream. At first she was sceptical, especially when I told her that North wanted me to stay the night, but finally she said if it was important then I had better stay. I called North and said that I was happy to go ahead.

The following Saturday afternoon I drove over to Ravenhurst. North greeted me at the door and said that we could begin immediately. He led me to a cellar door and down a flight of stairs to a small basement room lined with wooden lockers. Opening one of these with a key he extracted a white robe and asked me to remove my outer garments and shoes and socks and to put on the robe and a pair of leather sandals. I did as he asked while he dressed in similar fashion, except that his robe was of deep purple.

When we were ready he opened another locker and took out a candle in a pewter holder. Having lit this he beckoned to me to follow him, and we descended by another flight of stairs, stone this time, and walked along a cold stone-flagged corridor until we were standing in front of a heavy oak door. Handing me the candle, North took out a key and opened the door. As it swung back the draft blew the candle out. "Wait here," said North's voice in the darkness, "while I light the other candles." For a few moments I could see nothing, but emanating from the room on whose threshold I stood came an odor of some kind of incense mingled with a smell that made me think of rich draperies. Then the room began to fill with a soft light, as North lit a series of candles in sconces round the walls, and I saw that my sense of smell had not deceived me.

We were in a room, perhaps twenty feet by thirty, whose ceiling was beautifully vaulted in the manner of the crypt of a medieval church and whose far wall was hung with a velvet cloth of rich dark blue embroidered in silver with a pentagram within a hexagram and some Hebrew letters. In the middle of the room stood an altar, covered in a white cloth. On it was a candle, a dagger, a sword, a wand, and an incense burner.

North lit the candle, then placed the one he was holding beside it; he then lit the burner. Next he walked clockwise round the altar in a wide radius, unraveling as he did so a length of white thread which he laid on the floor to form a circle. When the circle was almost complete he left the two ends of the thread untied. He motioned to me to enter the circle, and then quickly followed. When we were both inside he tied the two ends of the thread together. "The circle of protection is now complete," he said. "Whatever happens you must remain within it until I give the word to leave."

He ordered me to stand facing the altar. Then, standing between me and the altar, with his back to me, he made a crossing movement with his right hand intoning as he did so, in a powerful, vibrant voice, the words: "Ateh, Malkuth, Ve Geburah, Ve Gedulah, Le Olahm, Amen."

Having done this he took a sword from the altar and traced a pentagram in the air, vibrating as he did so the Hebrew name of God "Yahweh". He then repeated the trading motion at each of the remaining three points of the compass, at which he vibrated respectively the god-names "Adonai", "Ehehieh" and "Agla".

When he was once again facing east, toward the altar, he remained for a few moments motionless and silent. Then he said, with the same rich intonation: "Before me Raphael, behind me Gabriel, on my right hand Michael, on my left hand Auriel. For around me flame the pentagrams and above me shines the six-rayed star." And then he repeated the formula with which he had begun the ceremony: "Ateh, Malkuth, Ve Geburah, Ve Gedulah, Le Olahm, Amen."

He then replaced the sword on the altar and took up a small alabaster jar of ointment into which he dipped his finger. He rubbed a little on my forehead, then returning to the altar he took up the wand and, facing me, said:

"Adepts of the Inner Planes, we salute you. There stands before you a candidate who has walked for long in the darkness and now seeks the gateway to the light. Once before he was turned from that gateway because he was unready. He now begs again for admission and waits on the threshold to submit once again to the test of worthiness."

He lifted the wand and held it aloft with both hands, then continued: "Let this wand be a bridge that shall take the candidate into the presence of those who would examine him."

He then stretched out his arm and slowly brought the wand down until it was touching the top of my head. At the moment of contact I seemed momentarily to lose consciousness, and when I regained it the walls of the temple and everything in it had dissolved into a swirling mist in which dim, fleeting figures were visible, moving swiftly and silently across my field of vision. Then the mist cleared and I saw that I was not in the temple but on a wild moorland on a cold, moonlit night with the wind lashing wildly at a few stunted trees. The dim figures had solidified into several men dressed in cowled robes, who trudged beside me along a stony path.

What followed was like a series of dim fragments of memory brought suddenly into sharp focus: a walk through a wood toward a fire whose light flickered between the dark tree trunks, the emergence into a clearing where the silhouette of a dark, robed figure was outlined against the flames, the feeling of many hands removing my clothes and dressing me in some animal-skin costume, with a mask over my face. In this condition I was brought before the robed figure and I now saw that he also wore a mask – a green face covered with leaves and surmounted by horns like those of an antelope. He raised his right hand and said in a resonant voice: *"Procul hinc abeste profani."* Then, placing his left hand on my head, he said: "You come before us to receive the final test. When we assemble again you will either be one of us or you will be dead and your soul will have vanished like the souls of the wild beast whose skin you wear."

Next I found myself running away from the fire and on to a bare hillside. At first I felt intensely alone; then I began to feel presences around and above me which now were mere misty suggestions of shapes, forming and dissolving rapidly, now more concrete manifestations which took on strange and repellent forms – a snake with a human head slithering across my path, a pool which bubbled and smoked like lava, an enormous jellyfish with a vast mouth at its centre. Yet these things dispersed and vanished as soon as I approached them. And their terror was alleviated by the sensing of other entities, less well-defined, but benevolent, sustaining, that hovered near at hand.

Then came the part that I had already relived so many times. Yet this time I knew that the end hung in the balance. Behind me and coming closer, I could hear the baying of hounds. Ahead there loomed up the abyss with the beckoning figures on the other side. Then there arrived the final, decisive moment. As I reached the edge the benevolent presences seemed to come together and I felt a surge of power lift me over the chasm. But I did not reach the other side. I hovered weightless above the abyss and looking back I realized that it was only a part of me that hung there. The rest, in its animal costume, still stood on the edge. It turned and faced its pursuers, and as it did so they stopped and fell back as though afraid.

Then I seemed to be falling, not into the abyss but somewhere else. I became dizzy and my surroundings dissolved into mist. For a long time I seemed to spin through space. Then I lost consciousness. When I regained it I was lying on the floor of the vaulted temple, within the magic circle, and North was leaning over me and helping me to my feet.

He told me to remain where I was and proceeded to perform the ritual with which he had opened the proceedings, after which he broke the circle and wound up the white thread. He turned toward me. "We must now close the temple," he said, and raising his right hand he intoned the words: "*Procul hinc abeste profani.*"

I rose, followed North out of the temple and changed into my ordinary clothes as though in a trance. A grandfather clock in the hall said five to eleven as we emerged into the upper part of the house. We had been in the temple for something like five hours. I had been in trance for most of that time, and I felt exhausted, as though everything I had experienced in my dream-like state had been real.

Over a light supper together I told North everything that I had experienced in the ritual. He listened attentively, and when I had finished he said: "The part when you came to the chasm is most significant. Instead of leaping across or falling you found a third way. Your body turned and boldly faced your pursuers, while your higher consciousness floated in space above the gap. You had placed yourself in the sphere of Daath, the sphere that floats in the abyss, the place from which you can look up to the world of the infinite or down to the material world, so that when you act in the world of everyday things you do so as a truly free and sovereign being. You passed the test triumphantly, but in your own way."

After we had finished eating, North showed me to my bedroom, and I sank gratefully into a deep sleep.

4

I awoke I the morning slowly, as I always do, stepping into waking consciousness like a bather venturing into a cold sea, advancing, retreating and advancing again. I opened my eyes on the unfamiliar room, became aware of its fresh, pleasant smell and the strangeness of the big, springy bed. As I took all this in I recaptured a feeling that I had not experienced for many years, the excitement of waking in a new environment, as it had been at the beginning of childhood holidays in Scotland and again on the first morning in my rooms at Oxford. Then, as now, I had the feeling of confronting a vista full of exciting possibility, of many roads stretching outward from that point in time and offering an infinite choice of adventures.

And yet this occasion was a bit different from the others. Then, the sensation of well-being had come from the mixture of the unfamiliar and the secure. The child, waking in a holiday bedroom, knows that he carries with him into the unknown future the cocoon of family life which prevents the unknown from becoming menacing. As we grow older we enlarge the cocoon with all the habits of an ordered existence and at the same time long for the unfamiliar. We blame our imprisonment on our wives, families, jobs, even our childhood conditioning, without realizing that the prison lies in our own minds, in our unwillingness to face the dark side of the unknown instead of merely being titillated by its pleasant aspects. The future that confronted me now was a mixture of light and dark, and I was able to behold it without wishing to draw back. I knew that I could no more remove the shadows that I could remove the passing clouds outside that now and then broke up the sunlight flooding in through the two big tall windows opposite the bed.

The room had obviously been decorated by Mrs. North. It bore the stamp of a woman with a sure visual sense. The delicate grey and white striped wallpaper was hung with prints and silhouettes. Between the two windows were six shelves of white china arranged against an orange background. At one end of the room was a fireplace with some logs in the grate, and on the marble mantlepiece was a pair of white porcelain birds and the figure of a colourful, pot-bellied Chinaman. He was leaning back and tossing some delicacy into his mouth. His merry serenity seemed to mock my serious thoughts of moment before. I was sure that had he spoken he would have said that there was no good and evil, only Yin and Yang, two complementary principles forming innumerable and every-changing permutations according to the law of the Tao, the quiet and irresistible flow of the universe. Perhaps his laughing face concealed the knowledge that his philosophy was too exalted for the Western world which he surveyed. His tranquil expression harmonized with the cooing of the woodpigeons outside in the park. Otherwise there was an unbroken silence until somewhere in the distance a church clock struck eight.

The sound of the chiming stirred some slightly uncomfortable memory which for a moment I could not pin down. Then it came back to me. During the night I had had a dream. It had begun with my walking down a broad ride in a beech wood. As I walked I heard something moving behind me but was afraid to turn around to see what it was. Then a clock started to chime – that was how I remembered the dream when I heard the other clock. It was chiming ten o'clock, and I was suddenly filled with a sense of urgency, not only to escape from whatever was behind me, but to catch a train, for the ride had mysteriously transformed itself into a station platform. The engine-driver was North, and as I leapt on to the train I heard him shout: "First stop the rose garden!" Then, after what seemed only a few seconds: "Here we are at the rose garden." Without being aware of any abrupt transition I found myself walking down a broad avenue of rose-trellises, which I recognized as part of the garden at Ravenhurst. At the end the avenue opened out into a round space in the middle of which was a stone pillar with a stone cherub on top and, surrounding the pillar, a circular wooden bench painted white. Sitting on the bench was a double of myself. The figure was reading a book, narrow shoulders hunched forward, long, thin head tilted at a slight angle, hands resting on knees and holding the book. One hand reached up and brushed the untidy, fairish hair in a gesture which I recognized as typical. As he read he occasionally looked up and began to mutter something, as though what he had read had sparked off a train of thought. Trying to remember the dream I had the impression that I had read all these thoughts with perfect clarity, though in my waking state I could remember nothing of them. I did remember, however, that this double and its thoughts struck me as being fairly absurd. As I watched, the double stood up in another characteristic movement and walked off with a slightly stiff gait.

I found myself in a different part of the garden, the walking down the main drive toward the house. As I approached the house there came rushing down the drive toward me the man from the College of Arms whom I had gone to see about the Wild Man. He wore an expression of intense terror, and as he flew past me he panted out in a frightened voice that he had just seen his double. I walked on toward the house expecting to see this other double, but instead what I saw approaching me was once again the double of myself. After that the dream became confused and faded into other dreams which I could not remember.

Thinking over the dream I remembered that I had sometimes wished that I could see myself as someone else would see me. It was almost a masochistic wish, for I was conscious of an awkwardness in my presence and personality which often made people ill at ease in my company. More than that, I had always felt that something set me apart from my fellow human beings. When I was a child this feeling had taken the form of a strange conviction that I was old beyond my apparent years, an old mind in a young body. Now it struck me that this conviction might have been child's unconscious realization that I had lived before.

My thoughts were interrupted by a soft knock at the door. I said: "Come in," and the maid, Jean, appeared with a tray. "Mr. North thought you might like some coffee," she said in a soft, country voice. She brought a pleasant kitchen smell with her as she set the tray down on a small table by the bed. On the tray was some rich, fragrant coffee in a white pot, a jug of cream, sugar, and a big cup and saucer. "Breakfast will be ready in about half an hour," she said as she left the room. I thanked her, drank the coffee luxuriously, then shaved and dressed.

Down I the dining room I found North already breakfasting, the Sunday newspaper spread out on the table beside him. He invited me to whatever I wanted from the sideboard. There was cereal, and bacon and eggs on a hot plate. I helped myself to first one, then the other, while we chatted about the morning news. The events reported were gloomy. The Vietnam war was at its height, and in the Middle East the Arabs and Israelis were rattling their sabres for another conflict. At home there was a balance of payments crisis, industrial trouble and a particularly nasty story about a multiple murder in Bradford. The murderer claimed that he had made a pact with the Devil, who had forced him to commit the crimes. In court the defense was pleading insanity.

"What do you make of that?" asked North as he poured out another cup of coffee for me. "Do you think the Devil might have had a hand in it?"

"Possibly," I replied, without quite knowing whether he was serious, "the idea of the Devil may have acted as a motivation..."

"And the Devil as an individual?"

"Do you believe in him as an individual?" I countered.

"It's an interesting question," he replied, "but perhaps not one for the breakfast table. Let's take a walk outside as it's a fine morning."

This time we took a different route and were soon walking along the edge of a large field bordered by beech wood. It was a still, sunny morning. Every now and then the North would stop to point out a bird or wild flower. I soon discovered that he had an extensive knowledge of natural history. After a while he returned the conversation we had started at breakfast.

"Of course the Devil isn't a person with horns and cloven feet and a tail. All the same, it's more sensible to think of him that way than to dismiss him altogether. The conventional Devil is symbolic of a real principle that exists in the universe – the principle of imbalance leading to disintegration."

He stopped and rested his hand against the side of a huge oak tree standing by itself beside a stile that we were about to cross.

"You see this oak. It is held together by two immense energies: the energy of force and the energy of form. Without the combination of the two the tree could not exist. The Jewish Kabbalists represent force and form as the two outside pillars of the Tree of Life. The third pillar, the middle, represents the balance between the two. Evil occurs whenever the two outer pillars are out of balance. So there are two kinds of imbalance.

"Look at it in human terms. All of us have a rational and an emotional side. If the rational side gets out of hand then we get a society where people become like machines, where science and technology expand at the expense of human values. If it goes the other way and the emotional side gets out of control then you get a phenomenon like Hitler. The Devil – let's talk about him as a person for convenience – the Devil delights in the pendulum swing from one extreme to the other. What he always seeks to prevent is the balanced mean. It is this balance that the true magician aims for. But when we talk about balance we don't mean the balance of a sloth hanging on the branch of a tree, but what Lemuel Johnstone in his book on magic describes as the laughing, joyful, moving balance of the dancer.

"Today we are erring on the rational side. The world we live in is becoming more and more mechanical, and the spirit of man is shriveling up as it is cut off from the springs of nature and the old values of truth and beauty. Somehow or other those values must be preserved, just as learning was preserved in the monasteries during the Dark Ages. But today it is not so much the world of learning that is in danger, or even the world of art and culture. It is the more ghostly things that are threatened, the hidden forces behind our civilization."

I realized now that the initiation I had been through the day before was only the beginning of my relationship with North. I began to understand that he was engaged on some great task in which I was to help him in a way that he had not yet defined.

"I maintain my temple here," he went on, "as one of a network of centres of light throughout the world. I work with a number of close friends, some of whom you will later meet. A few of them I have trained in magical techniques – the rest were already trained. Very few people are suitable material for such training, but you. . ." he turned and poked his pipe at me "you are one of them."

"And you are offering to train me?" I asked.

"Yes, indeed, I am offering, but only offering, not urging. When I have told you a bit more about what is involved then you can decide for yourself."

We walked on for a while in silence. We were now travelling along the edge of a small stream back in the direction of the house.

"Your initiation," North continued, "was on the unconscious level. Consciously, I should imagine that you are still a bit confused as to what magic is all about. So let's reduce it to its bare essentials. Basically what we are trying to do in magic is to use our imaginations and wills creatively in order to achieve an ideal. Now let us suppose that our ideal is to bring about a balance within ourselves. The first thing we have to do is to understand what it is that needs to be balanced, what forces in us are conflicting. Each of these forces is given a name and certain characteristics and images that are associated with it. We then build up a system of images which we can manipulate with our imaginations. And we become more skilled at this the more familiar we become with the system we are using. To signify the different stages of development in a person's mastery of the system we have a series of grades of initiation. Finally we have a set of rituals, some of which we use for initiation to the grades, some for invoking particular symbols within the system."

"But surely," I interrupted, "the magician invokes more than symbols. He invokes beings from other planes."

North nodded. "Every force within the human being has its counterpart in the cosmos. Therefore every time we call up something inside us we are calling up something in the universe as well. These cosmic forces are symbolized as beings from other planes. We see those forces in whatever shape is appropriate to our system of belief. An ancient Egyptian invokes a particular force and sees the goddess Isis. A Christian invokes the same force and sees the Virgin Mary. But these images exist not only in the imagination of the worshiper. Centuries of belief build up collective images which almost have a life of their own. This is why you often get a whole crowd of people seeing the same vision.

"But returning to the bricks and mortar of magic – to sum up, magic consists of four basic things: you have an ideal of some kind; you have a system of symbolism in which the ideal is enshrined; you have a series of grades; and finally you have a set of rituals. Now if you consider these elements you'll realize that people are using the principles of magic all the time without realizing it. Take a large American corporation for example. The employee carries with him the image of the perfect corporation man: efficient, hard-working, loyal, and decisive. This ideal is symbolized by the picture of a short-haired, smart-suited man in a chauffeured car, rushing from one important meeting to another. The grades on the ladder up to the height that he occupies are marked by ritualistic observances – the carpet on the floor of one's office, the acquisition of an extra secretary, the company car, the chauffeur and so on. The soldier, the civil servant, the Communist Party member all go through a similar process without realizing it. The difference between them and the true magician is that the magician uses the process consciously. He is the master of his symbols, instead of being controlled by them as so many people are today."

I had been listening so intently to what North was saying that I had been unaware that he had re-entered the garden of the house and were approaching the rose avenue. As we walked down it I was suddenly reminded of my dream, but one thing that struck me was that the roses were trained over a diagonally-crossing lattice framework instead of the series of widely-spaced bars, crossing vertically and horizontally, that I had seen in the dream.

What North had been saying about symbols gave me the opportunity to ask him what he made of the symbolism of the dream – the roses and the incident of the double. He listened thoughtfully while I recounted the dream, and by the time I had finished we were back in the house and sitting in his study.

"There are three things that stand out here," he said. "First the detail of the roses. Your unconscious mind seized on a place where roses grew, because roses have a special significance to you. The trellises on which the roses were growing took the form of crosses, in other words what you say was a disguised form of the old symbol of the Rose Cross, the badge of the Rosicrucian Brotherhood. This could be an echo from the past, or possibly a sign for the future.

"Secondly, the double of yourself. This is a sign that your unconscious mind has already progressed quite a long way along the road of magical attainment, for one of the things that happens during the training of a magician is that he sheds the shell of his old self with all its mechanical habits and conditioning. This shell is something that we go on building up all our lives. It becomes our conception of ourselves which is partly a reflection of how other people see us. Therefore everything we do or say or think, however trivial, helps to form this shell, and eventually in most cases the shell takes over and the spirit inside dies. That is what Christ meant when he said: 'Let the dead bury their dead.' And when he talks about being 'born again' he is speaking of the throwing off of the old conditioned self. You have already begun to do this, and what you saw sitting in the garden in your dream was that other self. From your new vantage point you were able to see this other self only as something slightly futile but for some people the same experience can be terrifying because for the first time they are seeing themselves with complete clarity, with all their faults, and that can be a difficult thing to face.

"And that brings me to the most remarkable feature of your dream, the incident of the herald running past you on the drive. This man did in fact come to see me. He had found out about the Brotherhood of the Wild Men through his heraldic studies and, like you, had been directed to me to find out more about it. I saw at once that he did not have the qualities for magical work, so I revealed nothing to him that he did not know already. What happened after he left me I don't know. He had come on foot to the house as his car had broken down in the village, and it's possible that something happened on his walk back. This house and its grounds have one or two places where there are strange vibrations. The rotunda in the rose garden is one of them. Possibly he may have passed one of these places and seen what the Germans call a *Doppelgänger*, a reflection of himself. But in his case the experience was too much for him and he fled. Of course..." He paused and filled his pipe before going on. "Of course there are various other things that cause people to see reflections of themselves. Sometimes what one is seeing is an independent being from another plane who takes on the characteristics of the person who sees it. This is said to happen in the Jewish tradition of the golem." He went on to explain that the golem is creature formed out of earth and endowed with life through a magical Kabbalistic formula. "The creation of a golem is usually considered to be an act of evil sorcery, and you'll find very few Jewish Kabbalists who will even talk about it. But there are stories of people who have seen golems that appeared as mirror images of themselves."

"Is it possible," I asked, "according to the tradition, for the golem to become a human being."

"No, the golem is a barren creature who can never develop into anything of a higher order. In order to set the golem in motion the magician has to transfer to the creature a fragment of his, or someone else's soul – but only a fragment, which by itself is sterile. Hence the golem is almost by definition unbalanced, and the power that motivates him usually comes from the lower realms. The creation of a golem is an operation that calls for great skill, as only an adept of the highest order, either good or evil, can carry it out and control the golem. Very few people have written authoritatively about the golem, but there is one who has. Have you heard of Gustav Meyrink?"

"I believe so. Wasn't he a banker turned occult novelist?"

North nodded. "He was the illegitimate son of an actress and a German aristocrat. He spent his formative years among the German-speaking community in Prague, which is a city steeped in occult tradition. Meyrink was a member of a secret occult lodge and knew what he was talking about. I have a book of his which you can borrow – if I can find it."

He stood up and walked to the book-lined wall opposite the fireplace where he ran his finger across the spines of the books until he found what he was looking for. He came back holding a small volume which he handed to me. "I have not read it properly," he said, "as my German is very poor, but I shouldn't think you'll have any trouble with it. I believe you told me your German was reasonably good."

I nodded as I took the book and looked at the title on the cloth spine: *Der Golem*. I turned over the first few pages, and the sight of the German Gothic lettering, in its tightly-set ranks with its little spikes and curls, stirred a pleasant memory. Like the taste of black cherry jam and the smell of strong coffee brewing, it reminded me of holidays in the Black Forest and along the Rhine. I thanked North and said that it was time for me to go as Sally was expecting me back for lunch. Before I went he handed me several other books to borrow. One in particular, on magical training, he recommended me to study carefully. We arranged that I should call again in ten days.

During the next few days I read the book on magic, and it

recommended the keeping of a "magical diary" in which dreams and the success of visualization exercises were to be recorded. I began to try some of the exercises and dream-recalling and to make records in a large notebook with a red cover which I had bought for the purpose. At first my attempts resulted in a confused jumble of dissociated images. Then I began to see patterns in the images. Certain colours and shapes went together. I found myself entering different levels, each of which had its own set of symbols, and I learned to use the Tree of Life as a map for finding my way from one level to another and for interpreting what I saw.

I went to see North on the evening arranged and, without being asked, showed him the diary. He read it with approval, made a few criticisms and offered some suggestions as to how I could overcome certain difficulties I had come across. I went to see him again two weeks later, then again the following fortnight. Without making any conscious agreement we had entered into the relationship of teacher and pupil. Our fortnightly meetings became regular and took place either at Ravenhurst or at his London flat.

Sometimes as I travelled to and from London on the train or walked up the steep streets of Gorehamstead to my house I found the world around me no less real or unreal than the worlds I visited during my meditations. Everything that happened to me I found myself experiencing with a kind of detachment, and this must have showed in my behaviour, for Sally noticed a change in me. "I sometimes wish," she said to me one evening, "that you had never met this mad guru of yours, this Gilbert North."

"Really, Sally!" I protested. "It's hardly fair to call Gilbert a mad guru."

"Well, he seems to be filling your head with some very strange ideas, and lately you've become a different person."

"What kind of person?" I asked.

"You've become distracted. It's as though you were living with half of you in another world."

When I told North about this conversation he nodded thoughtfully and said: "Yes, I can understand what she means. The hardest part about any spiritual training is coming down to earth again afterwards. The Zen people put it very well. They say that before you start on your training mountains are mountains and trees are trees. During mystical experience mountains are no longer mountains and trees are no longer trees. Then afterwards mountains are mountains and trees are trees again, but in a different way. You have not quite mastered the art of coming back into the third state, which is why your wife feels uncomfortable. The point is you must not give up doing all the things that you used to do. Laugh, get drunk occasionally, even get angry or aggressive. You can cause yourself and other people no harm as long as you keep the centre of your being calm and conscious." I thought of the laughing Chinaman on the mantelpiece upstairs. He had the secret of keeping his spirit turned to heaven and his feet firmly on the ground.

"Women," North went on, "have different approach to these things from men. The difference between men and women on the spiritual level is that women are born complete and spend their lives giving out strength from that completeness. Men, on the other hand, are born incomplete and have to struggle to find completeness. It's a mistake for a man to expect a woman to go with him in his search. Equally, a woman cannot expect her man to remain static. She must allow him to go ahead and commit whatever follies are necessary for his development. If only the sexes would value and honour each other's roles there would be much less marital unhappiness."

"Would you say," I asked, "that the woman's role was a passive one?"

"No, that would be the wrong way of putting it. Look at it this way. If you are trying to move a weight by means of a lever pressing against a fulcrum it is the fulcrum, the fixed point, that really does the work. Well, woman is in a sense the fulcrum. We men merely manipulate the lever. I'd like to meet your wife. Bring her and your son over for tea some time."

So a couple of weeks after the "mad guru" conversation with Sally I took up North's invitation and drove with her and Mark to Ravenhurst for tea. We were met at the door by North's wife Diana. She was a tall, aristocratic-looking woman with greying hair that must once have been raven black. Her long face, strong and finely shaped, had a trace of something Latin or perhaps Semitic about it. It was the sort of face that one expects to see framed by the lintel and pillars of an Egyptian temple instead of by the doorway of an English country house.

"You must be Paul and Sally," she said in a strong, warm voice.

"And I guess this is Mark." She reached down to take Mark's hand. "How nice that you are all here. Gilbert is waiting in the drawing room."

As I had expected the Norths quickly won Sally over with their charm. After tea Diana offered to show Sally around the house, while Gilbert and I and Mark took a walk in the garden.

At home in the evening, when Sally and I were having supper after Mark had gone to bed, she was quiet and pensive. Then, when I asked her how she and Diana had got on, she suddenly began to talk excitedly, her eyes bright.

"Oh Paul, they are both such wonderful, extraordinary people. I had no idea ... I've never met a woman like Diana before, and yet we spoke so freely to each other that it was as though I had known her all my life. She talked a lot about the roles of the sexes in the work that they do, and she said such amazing, wise things – about how men have to go by long, roundabout routes, like through a labyrinth, before they come back to the centre where they really belong, and how women know how to keep the centre strong and vital. She showed me some old books of alchemy with strange, marvellous pictures of couples working together at furnaces or gathering dew or making love in watery grottoes. She said that those old alchemists knew that sex underlies all of nature and that only when both sexes work in unison can the 'Great Work', as she called it, be accomplished."

"And did she say anything about me and my work with Gilbert?"

"Yes, she said it's all part of the labyrinth that you have to go through to reach the centre. Oh ... and she said something a bit mysterious – that you might find as you go along that certain things are not what they seem, but that you must trust that you are on the right course. And she also said that one day you would have a special part to play in the great work, but meanwhile you have some way to go on your own." She reached out and put a hand on mine. "Darling, I was silly to be so sceptical about Gilbert. I won't say another word against him."

And so, with Sally's blessing, North's teaching progressed, and I found myself slowly picking up something of his ability to reach upwards into hidden realms without losing touch with the ground. The summer passed pleasantly. In August I took Sally and Mark for a holiday in Cornwall and on my return decided to tackle *Der Golem* which had lain unread on the desk in my little study upstairs at the back of the house. One fine Sunday afternoon in September I took it out into the garden and sat down in the shade of the big hawthorn tree to read it.

I was immediately transported into the unfamiliar world of the Old Jewish quarter in Prague, a bizarre yet vividly real world of tall old houses thrusting crookedly up from cobbled alleyways and dark courtyards. In this enclosed environment life moved much as it had done since the Middle Ages. The character of the inhabitants had the tight strength of a root grown in upon itself, and the air they breathed was full of the dust and ghosts of the past. As I read Meyrink's description of this world I knew that I was in contact with a powerful intellect which had delved deeply into the dark side of the human mind and knew the forces that lurk there with a more than academic knowledge.

In such a world as he described folk traditions had a power that was lacking in less enclosed communities. A part of the ghetto's folklore was the figure of the golem, and as I read about the legend a particular passage caused me to stop and read it over again.:

"As on days of close weather the electrical tension increases to an unbearable degree and finally gives birth to lightning, could it not also be the case that the continual accumulation of those never-changing thoughts that poison the air of the ghetto could occasionally cause a sudden eruption—a spiritual explosion which drives our dream consciousness out of the daylight to create a ghost which in action, conduct and appearance would express the collective soul of the community to someone who understood the secret language of form?

"And as some kinds of manifestation give warning of a lightning storm, so here certain grim portents betray the threatening emergence of that phantom into the realm of fact."

Despite the warm sunshine that fell across the lawn in front of me, and all the sounds of a peaceful September afternoon, I could not repress a chill sensation that crept over me as I read Meyrink's words. The gulf between a quiet garden in England and the dark, huddled world of the Prague ghetto seemed suddenly to narrow to a hair's breadth. Even when Sally came out a few moments later with a tea tray and we talked of other things, I could not entirely banish a feeling of disquiet from my mind.

Over the next few days I kept being reminded of the passage. The weather started to lose its clear, late-summer freshness and become heavy, close, and overcast. Everyone seemed to become irritable, and one could sense a groundswell of tension that appeared to be affecting people's behaviour everywhere. Strange little incidents added to this feeling. One day, walking through the back streets of Covent Garden I noticed the bodies of dozens of dead and mutilated pigeons strewn about on the ground. I later heard that none of the locals could explain it. The incident never reached the press, but other strange happenings did. In Birmingham a horde of unusually ferocious rats had terrorized an entire street, and several people had been badly bitten. In other parts of the country there had been several cases of placid domestic pets turning suddenly aggressive. There also seemed to be an unusual number of reports of crimes of violence. Meyrink's words kept coming back more and more insistently to my mind. "Certain grim portents betray the threatening emergence of that phantom into the realm of fact."

One night I had a dream which seemed to be connected with these events. I saw a heap of corpses, severed limbs and heads. Over the heap a figure was walking, a stooping figure dressed in a tattered garment which hung around him in wisps like pieces of cobweb. As he came closer I saw that his face was the colour and texture of clay. His eyes resembled those of a fish. On his forehead were engraved three Hebrew letters.

When I next saw North I told him about the dream, about the passage in the book and about my feeling that they were connected with the general tension of the past few days.

We were sitting in his study, and when I had finished telling him, he walked over to his desk and wrote something on a piece of paper with a pencil. Then he came back and handed me the paper. On it were written the Hebrew letters *aleph, mem* and *teth.*

"Were those," he asked, "the letters you saw engraved o the forehead of the figure in your dream?"

I looked at them carefully. "It's difficult to be sure," I said, "but I think so."

"At any rate, you're quite sure the letters you saw where Hebrew letters and that there were three of them?"

"Oh yes, I'm quite sure of that."

"In that case," said North, "we can be fairly certain that what you saw was a golem. The letters are roughly equivalent to the English A, M, and T. They mean 'firmness'. The Hebrew tradition says that if the golem gets out of hand then you can put an end to him by erasing the first letter, leaving the root MT which means 'death'. The trouble is we don't know if a golem has been created or whether what you saw was perhaps a premonition. And even if we did know there would be nothing we could do at this stage. A golem is like a pustule caused by an accumulation of poison. You have to get rid of the poison before you can destroy its outward symptom. All we can do is wait and see what happens."

He cast the paper into the log fire burning in the grate. The three Hebrew letters stood out momentarily before the paper blackened and curled up in the flames.

5

As it turned out we did not have to wait very long. Two days after my conversation with North I received a telephone call at the office from an old Oxford friend, Tim Bassett, who was now an archaeologist attached to the Oxford City and County Museum. He had now become one of the many contacts through whom I kept in touch with what was going on in the world of archaeology. On this occasion he was telephoning to tell me that he was engaged on some emergency excavations in Oxford which he thought might make a good article. It sounded interesting, so I thanked him and said that I would come the following day. As it happened there were some new exhibits at the Ashmolean Museum that I had been meaning to look at, so I planned to do both jobs the same day and then spend the night in my old college. I rang the college steward to book a room, and began to look forward to the prospect of a day in my old university town.

I arrived at mid-morning the following day, having driven from home, and found on arrival that I had been given a room on a staircase where I had lived as an undergraduate. I turned into the doorway, and as I sniffed the familiar smell of old woodwork and saw the names of the coming year's undergraduates freshly painted over the doors of the rooms on the ground floor, I wondered whether my old scout, Chudley, would still be there. He had always been something of a legend. Nobody knew quite how old he was, but he had certainly been there since just after the First World War, for he remembered how some young Tory bloods had run riot in the college the night of the election when Lloyd George was returned to power.

I mounted the worn steps of the wooden stairway with its heavy balustrade to the first floor where the scout's pantry was – an unusual feature since the pantry was usually on the ground floor. I looked round the door, and there he was, sitting over coffee with the woman who helped him to clean the rooms. He appeared as he had always done: a lean, eternally young face looking out from beneath a mass of white hair.

"Well, bless my soul!" he said when he saw me. "How are you, Sir?"

"Do you know, when they told me you were staying the night here the name didn't ring any bell, but now it all comes back. You shared with Mr. Campbell, didn't you? How is Mr. Campbell?"

I shook my head. "Haven't seen him for years, I'm afraid. We rather lost touch." Chudley nodded. "I expect you've got lots of new friends now – and married I shouldn't wonder."

"Yes," I said, "with a small son."

"Goodness me! It seems only yesterday you were here. Do you enjoy coming back?"

"Very much. I enjoyed my time here."

He nodded again. "Yes, it's the happiest time of your life, isn't it? Or so they say. Will you stay for a cup of coffee?"

I said no thank you, for I had arranged to go to the excavation headquarters at eleven o'clock. I left my suitcase in my room and made my way to the terrace house near Folly Bridge where the excavation committee had its headquarters.

I had known the director of excavations, Tim Bassett, slightly as an undergraduate and found that, like Chudley, he had changed little. He was a solidly built person with dark hair, heavy eyebrows and a thick, untidy beard. He led me to a small office at the back of the building on the first floor, strewn with maps and pieces of pottery. He began by pouring out some coffee, and this time I agreed to have some.

When we were seated with the steaming mugs on the table beside us he began to explain what his team had been doing. For many years the secrets of Oxford's early history had lain undisturbed beneath the colleges to the east and the rather seedy but not unromantic residential district to the west. Most of the latter has long since given way to a vast shopping centre, but I can remember it as it was: a region of poky lodging houses, junk shops and small corner grocers. Between the bulldozers and the builders the archaeologists had moved in, and the area had yielded a rich harvest of finds: Saxon walls, medieval pottery, and, most dramatic of all, the remains of a great Franciscan church.

"The church," explained Tim, "contained some very interesting objects. There was this, for instance." And he showed me a photograph of a headless and armless stone figure. "Probably a statuette of St. James of Compostella. I can't show you the original because it's been taken to a museum for closer analysis. Then of course there's all the pottery." He opened a cupboard and took out some earthenware jugs. "These are the most complete specimens, but there are stacks of sherds in our storeroom downstairs." He put the pots back after I had looked at them, and rummaged in another cupboard. "I don't think there's anything more that you would find particularly exciting." Then he saw something and reached into the cupboard. "Except perhaps this." He had brought out a small marble container about the size and shape of a cigar box, its lid engraved with a cross, which he put on the table. "This we found the other day," he explained, "buried under some rubble in the north transept of the church." He opened the lid and lifted away a few shreds of what had once been a silk cloth, revealing a circular medallion made of lead. In the centre was engraved a curious linear symbol which I did not recognize, and around the edge were what appeared to be Hebrew letters. He held it up, and on the obverse side was a five-pointed star.

"Curious thing to find in a church, isn't it?" he said. I took it and was examining it when one of the excavators, a young girl, opened the door and said that some rather interesting pottery had just been brought in from a site in St. Aldate's.

"Thank you Maggie," Tim said. "Let's go and look at it shall, we Paul?" He put the box away in the cupboard again, and, as an afterthought, gave me a photograph of the object to take away with me. Then he ushered me down to a room on the ground floor where two young men were busy washing fragments of pottery at a sink. One of them handed him a piece of vase or jug which he took to the window to examine in the light.

"Curious," he said as his practised eye took in the contours. "It's a bit like some that we found near the church." And he picked up another piece from a table. "But, you see, the rim is fractionally different." Then he launched into a short lecture on the local kilns and their various designs. "We'll have a closer look at that lot after lunch," he said finally. "Would you like to join us?"

I agreed, and fifteen minutes later we were sitting in a nearby pub over shepherd's pie and bitter – Tim, myself, and three of the excavators. That lunch stands our vividly in my memory. I later had reason to make great efforts to call to mind how Tim had looked and behaved as we sat in the low-ceilinged, brown-panelled bar of the old pub off the High Street.

Was it imagination, or had I felt some premonition as I said goodbye to him outside the pub? At any rate I remember the rest of the day a good deal less clearly. But I must try to describe the evening in view of what happened later. Having spent the afternoon at the Ashmolean Museum I went at seven o'clock to the senior common room of the college to have a sherry before dinner. A number of dons were already gathered there. I recognized the tall figure of Kramer, the historian, with his thin, sensitive, Jewish face; the tiny, bird-like Dr. Matthew hopping about excitedly while talking to the bland and plump college chaplain, John Wakefield. The Master, Dr. Lionel Hardwick, was there too, a large man with a handsome grey head.

I was standing wondering who to talk to when my old philosophy tutor, Rupert Slade, came up to me. He was a tall man with a square, rather florid face and the most piercing eyes I have ever known. Many pupils had wilted beneath their pale blue glare, but this time the expression in them was friendly, and he greeted me warmly.

"Nice to see you again, Cairns," he said. "What brings you to Oxford?"

I explained about the excavations, and as I was doing so the Master came up to us, and I broke off while Slade introduced me to him.

"Ah yes," he said, nodding his powerful, leonine head. "You were here about seven years ago weren't you?"

"Correct," I replied, impressed by his memory. I had hardly spoken to him more than a couple of times during my whole three years at the college.

"Did I hear you talking about the excavations?" he asked. His voice was deep and mellow.

"Yes, that's right. I'm writing them up for my magazine."

"How interesting. Tell me, have they found any more significant objects recently? The last I heard about was that statue of St. James of Compostella."

"Yes. I was shown a rather fascinating thing this morning." And I told him about the medallion with the strange characters.

He seemed intrigued and was about to ask me more about it when somebody said that it was time for dinner, and there was a general move toward the door. We reassembled in the Hall, and I found myself sitting between a young law tutor and the chaplain. What we talked about I cannot remember, but I do remember the conversation that started later on in the common room when we were seated around a table over port. This time I found myself between the Master and Slade, the philosophy tutor. Somehow we had got on to the subject of witches, and Slade was telling a story about a friend of his at Cambridge who had come into conflict with an eccentric middle-aged lady named Muriel Quinn, who had written a number of books on witchcraft.

"You see, Mrs. Quinn," he explained "was in her own way quite a scholarly woman, and my friend arranged for her to give a course of extra-mural lectures. But there was some disagreement over her fee, and she hinted that unless she got the amount she wanted she would not be above the exercise of a little witchcraft. Eventually they came to a compromise, so my friend never found out if she was capable of carrying out her threat." His tone of voice as he told this story suggested amused scepticism.

"Tell me," I asked him, "would a hardened Oxford philosopher like yourself ever admit that there might be something in all this?"

"Witchcraft?" he said. "Certainly there's something in it if you happen to believe in it. If an African witch doctor tells a tribesman that he is going to die, the poor fellow does die because he believes in the witch doctor's magic. It's the same with all of these things – belief justifies itself."

At this point the Master intervened. "I'm afraid," he declared, "I hold the unfashionable view that there are supernatural forces. I also believe that there are some people who know how to tap them."

"But surely," broke in Dr. Matthew in his rather high-pitched voice, "it's as Rupert says: the people you speak of can only tap the forces because other people believe they can. In other words the forces are within the mind."

"Exactly," said Slade. "It's all a matter of conditioning. The Druid and the African witch doctor live in an environment where one has to believe in magical forces as an opiate against the uncertainties of nature. It's comforting to think that your magician can bring on the rain or cure an illness. But how can a person believe in magic when he lives in a modern bungalow with electricity and hot and cold water and a television to keep him happy?"

"You're quite wrong," said the chaplain quietly. "Before I came to this college I was curate in a modern housing estate near Birmingham. And let me tell you that for every Christian or agnostic there were a dozen believers in every other outlandish cult you can imagine – and that included a witches' coven. They were quite a harmless lot. They had a penchant, I was told, for drinking cream sherry during their rites. But I have heard of one or two groups that are not quite so harmless."

"Black magic?" asked Slade, smiling.

"Call it that if you like," said the chaplain, unperturbed by the other's cynicism. "I agree with the Master. There are supernatural forces and absolutes of good and evil. There is war in Heaven. Michael and his angels are fighting against the Dragon."

"And who is wining?" I asked.

"I fear that the Dragon is winning this round," Wakefield replied. "We seem to be passing through an era with more than its fair share of evil."

"Console yourself, John," said the Master, "with another glass of port." And he slid the decanter across the polished surface of the table.

After that the conversation drifted on to other topics, and port gave way to coffee and then brandy. I went to bed at midnight having drunk rather too much and slept badly as a result.

In the morning I drove back to London and arrived at the office at about eleven o'clock. On looking through my notes I found that there were a few questions I had forgotten to ask about the excavations, so I telephoned the office at Folly Bridge to speak to Tim Bassett. It was girl, Maggie, who answered.

"But haven't you heard?" she said. "There's been the most awful tragedy. Tim was killed yesterday in a car crash. He was on his way to take some things to the museum. He was driving home up the Banbury Road when a lorry came out from a side turning and he ran smack into it. He must have been going a fearful speed because the lorry driver said that he saw Tim coming, but thought he had plenty of time to get clear. The funny thing was that one of the objects was later found to be missing from the car – that medallion from the Greyfriars church."

I said how sorry I was about the news, and put down the telephone receiver. I remained for the rest of the morning in a state of shock. At first I thought only of the untimely loss of a friend through a tragic accident. Then a strange question began to nag at my mind. Had it really been an accident? There was little to suggest otherwise, but somehow an instinctive doubt troubled me.

I was too distracted to work, and in the middle of the afternoon I explained the situation to the editor, who immediately suggested that I go home. But some instinct told me to go and see North first. I tried to telephone him, but discovered that the line was out of order. So I decided to chance a visit. I had on my desk a selection of photographs that Tim had given me, and two of them showed the obverse and reverse sides of the medallion. A second impulse caused me to slip these into my briefcase. I knew that North stayed in London at that time of year.

To my great relief North was at home when I arrived at his flat. It was in an early Victorian building and was furnished and decorated with the same taste as his country house. In the drawing room a large armchair was drawn up before an electric fire. Beside it on the floor was a tea tray and several piles of books, some lying open, some with pages marked by slips of paper. I cleared some more books from the seat of a sofa and sat down while he fetched another cup.

"Well," he said, while he poured out the tea, "I can tell that something is on your mind."

I told him the events of the previous day, and when I had finished he said: "Well, let's have a look at this talisman of yours."

I handed him the photographs that I had brought with me, and as he examined them his expression grew more serious.

"Do you realize what this is?" he asked quietly, look up at me.

I shook my head.

"It's the Talisman of Bael. Does that mean anything to you?"

"No, I'm afraid not."

"Bael is a high-ranking demon, and this is an ancient talisman of great power that commands his obedience. Since it was made it has been used almost entirely for bad purposes and so has gathered about it an aura of evil. During the Middle Ages it was responsible for starting many wars, plagues, and other misfortunes. Then suddenly it mysteriously disappeared—no one knew where. Well now, thanks to your unfortunate friend Bassett, we know what happened. The

Franciscan friars got a hold of it and, realizing its power, bound it with magical seals and buried it under the floor of their church. At the Reformation the church was destroyed, leaving the talisman buried under the rubble where it might have stayed but for the discovery of the church's remains by archaeologists. In view of what has happened it would have been better if that excavation had never taken place."

"You think that someone has stolen it, realizing its evil power?"

"Undoubtedly, but who? And how did he find out so quickly that it had been unearthed? There are probably not more than half a dozen people in the world who know of that talisman, yet within twenty-four hours of its being dug up someone engineers a car accident for Bassett and steals the thing. The find had not yet been reported in the national press, so whoever stole it must have had inside information. The important question is: how high an adept is he? This could affect the amount of harm done by the talisman when the thief decides to get up to some mischief with it."

North was silent for a few moments, chewing thoughtfully at his empty pipe. Then he asked: "Did anyone witness the accident?"

"No, only the driver of the lorry. He was in such a state of shock, poor man, that he couldn't give a very coherent account of it, but there was one curious detail in his statement. Evidently he swears that there was another person in the car. Yet the car was a complete write-off, and no passenger would have had the slightest chance of survival."

North sat bolt upright in his chair. "This puts a different complexion on the matter," he said. "It's more serious than I thought."

"How do you mean?" I asked.

"The passenger that the lorry-driver saw must have been a conjuration sent for the purpose of causing the crash."

Before I had met North this suggestion would have been too much for my credulity. Now I took it in my stride.

"You mean," I said, "that the thief sent a ghost to help him steal the talisman."

North shook his head. "Not a ghost. The average ghost would not be controllable in that way. No, this was something altogether more powerful."

"You mean..."

"Yes," said North, finishing what was on the tip of my tongue, "A golem. And I know of only one man in this country capable of producing one. L.O.Q. It must be he."

We sat in silence while North slowly filled his pipe, pushing the tobacco into the bowl with thoughtful movements of his powerful fingers. At length he lit up and said, between puffs:

"There are certain things that we have in our favour. The Talisman of Bael is one that can only be used twice a year at the times of the equinoxes when the currents of power on the Inner Planes are at their strongest. The next opportunity to use it will be at the autumn equinox. We must be ready then."

"What do you propose to do?" I asked. I was alarmed by his use of the word "we". What could I possibly do to help?

"There's only one thing we can do," he said. "We can't get the talisman back. There's no hope of that. But we have to stop it being used for an evil purpose. So the only course that we can take is to send out a magical current that will counteract the emanations of the talisman. If we fail the current will strike us, but if we succeed it will flow back to L.O.Q. and, with any luck, destroy him."

There was an unusual touch of ruthlessness in his voice as he said this, but then we were dealing with an enemy who now had it in his power to perform miracles of evil. With such an enemy loose there could be no question of neutrality. To know the facts was to be committed to action against the evil. I realized all this, yet still I was frightened of being asked for my help by North.

"Another thing we have in our favour," he went on, "is that L.O.Q. is unaware that we know of the existence of the talisman – at least I can think of no way he could have found out. This means that we can take him by surprise. And our final trump card is the fact that I have the Talisman of Althotas which we can sue as a weapon."

"Is it stronger," I asked, "than the other talisman?"

"That I don't know," North replied, "and on the relative strengths of the two may depend the success or failure of our operation. It's a risk that may even put our lives in danger. Are you willing to take that risk by helping me?"

I had already made up my mind to agree, but as I said yes I had to conceal the shiver of fear that ran through me.

"Good," said North. "Now, it's ten to one that L.O.Q. will begin using the talisman at dawn on the 22nd of September, the autumn equinox, which is three weeks away. We shall immediately block the currents that he is sending out, and he will sense the interference and send one of his minions to destroy the source. Then it will be a trial of strength between us and whatever entity he sends."

"But surely," I said, "that means that even if L.O.Q. loses the fight he will have found out that you have the talisman and will return to the attack."

North nodded. "Yes, there is that risk, but we can guard against it by operating not from my temple but from some other spot which he would not associate with me. The entity he sends would remember me if he met me again, but would not be able to reveal my identity to L.O.Q. after only one encounter." He stood up and put his hand on my shoulder. "We have three weeks," he said "until the day. Meanwhile I shall get my talisman out from its cold storage. Come to my house early on the evening of the 21st."

He saw me to the door of the flat, and I left with a mixture of conflicting feelings. I was eager to help North and flattered that he should have asked me but at the same time I wondered if it was right for me to risk my sanity and even possible my life when I had a wife and child who were dependent on me. Conscience makes cowards of us all. I decided that Sally could not possibly understand my willingness to take such a risk and that it would be best not to tell her about it but to explain my visit to North by saying that I was going to stay with him as part of a harmless experiment the purpose of which I did not yet know.

I had never deceived Sally before, and the consciousness that I was doing so now - however excusable my reasons - added a chill feeling of guilt to my growing apprehension in the weeks that followed. With a kind of desperation I dreaded and yet longed for the eve of the equinox to arrive, and it was almost with relief that I set out for North's house when the appointed day came.

Twilight was falling as I drove to Ravenhurst, and though the trees and hedgerows were still green there was a premature autumn coldness in the air. The wind was snatching at the trees and sending the clouds hurrying across a sky the colour of grey ice. I felt a creeping sense of foreboding combined with a feeling of excitement.

It was approaching seven o'clock when I arrived at Ravenhurst. The maid answered the door and showed me into the study where North was sitting waiting for me in front of a blazing fire. He rose as I came in and beckoned me to the chair on the opposite side. The warmth of the fire and his presence calmed me down a bit and I began almost to forget the purpose of my visit. North was in no hurry to remind me, and for half an hour we sat and smoked cigars while he talked in a relaxed way about the problems of running a country estate and contending with the depredations of elm disease and the tax man.

At length he tossed the end of his cigar into the fire and stood up. "You must be hungry," he said. "Let's go and have something to eat." We went into the dining room and sat down to a meal of soup, cold chicken, and salad, which we ate in comparative silence. North seemed to be gathering strength for the evening's ordeal. Afterward, we returned to the study and sat for a while in front of the fire with coffee. North had not offered me any alcohol during the evening. I could guess the reason why. We had to have our wits about us for the job ahead.

Finally, at eleven o'clock, North stood up. "Time we were off," he said. "We'd better go in two cars in case something goes wrong with one of them. You follow me. The place is about twenty minute's drive from here."

From a corner of the room he picked up two pieces of luggage. One was a small stout leather suitcase. The other was a rather flashy travelling bag with the name of a well known airline on the side. It seemed an incongruous object to be taking on an expedition such as ours. North explained that it contained refreshments. "We may need our strength restored later on," he said. The other bag, he added, contained magical impedimenta and the all-important talisman. North could be almost casually practical at times. He would have carried the Holy Grail in an airline bag if it fitted in. But the same practicality also sometimes caused him to go to immense trouble to get exactly the result he wanted. It was for this reason that for his transport he carefully maintained the old Rolls-Royce shooting-brake that was waiting outside the front door.

"On an occasion like this a reliable car comes in useful," he commented, opening the back and loading in his two pieces of luggage. "Now follow me closely and you'll be all right. I'll keep an eye on you in my mirror to make sure you're behind."

We mounted the cars, drove off and took the road westward through Coombe Raven. As we passed the pub the last customers were leaving the red-lit saloon bar with sounds of laughter and good cheer. At that moment I longed to be a part of that cosy conviviality, but I put such thoughts away and followed the rear lights of the Rolls-Royce out into the country. Half a mile past the village we turned north and for several miles followed twisty side roads flanked by high hedges or banks of trees. Once a deer leapt across my headlights and vanished into the trees. It gave me a start and made me swerve slightly.

At length North slowed down, and we pulled up on a grassy expanse to the right of the road. Leaving the cars unlocked in case we should have to make a quick retreat, we walked away from the road and were soon following a path over a stretch of open land fringed with scrub and bracken. In spite of the bright moonlight the path was difficult to follow, but North evidently knew the way and did not hesitate.

"This path," he said, breaking the silence, "has been in use since the Stone Age. Further north it joins up with the Icknield Way. The place we are heading for is one of the ancient temple sites of this region."

After we had walked about another quarter of a mile I saw that we were on a shallow ridge that sloped downward ahead of us and flattened out into woodland. On the left a small platform of land jutted out of the west side of the ridge, and on it grew a clump of oak trees. I guessed that this was our destination. North soon confirmed my thoughts and added: "These old Stone-Age folk were more sophisticated than most people realize. They had knowledge and skills that are forgotten today." By now we were standing on the site, and I saw that the trees formed a ring. "Take this place, for instance," North went on and pointed to the ground. "Below here is a spring. They usually built their temples where there was underground water because of the beneficial influences that came from it. Their temples were places of healing as well as worship and contemplation, and they used their skill in water-divining to seek out these spots. Can you feel the power of this place?"

I stood still and tried to make my senses receptive, but at length I had to shake my head and admit that I could feel nothing. North showed no surprise. "That's because your finer faculties have been blunted by so-called civilized living. If you lived closer to nature it would be different. Animals are far more sensitive than we are to invisible influences. Cows, for instance, often seek out places where there is underground water when they are about to give birth. And during the Peninsular War some of Wellington's soldiers used to sleep on places where a cow had given birth because they found it relieved rheumatism."

I listened with fascination as North went on talking about the lost wisdom of the Stone-age people and describing their way of life. As he talked I began to feel an inkling of what I had failed to sense before. It was as though I had entered an empty house whose absent owner's personality lingered there invisibly. It was a strong and rough, but benevolent, personality whose presence sustained and calmed me and put me in a more resolute mood.

North must have noticed the change in me, for he picked up the suitcase and said: "It's time to get to work."

He then began a procedure similar to the one I had witnessed in the temple. Only this time the altar was a stone block rising from the middle of the clearing, a lichen-covered boulder with a crudely flattened top, put there, North told me, by the Stone-Age worshipers. Instead of a thread to form the circle of protection, he used a length of stout rope. When the circle was complete and we were standing inside he extracted from the bag the magical implements of sword, wand, dish, and chalice. The sword was a short, practical-looking weapon with round pommels on the guard of the hilt. The wand was of wood and formed into the shape of a lotus bud at one end. The two vessels were simple objects, made of pewter. He also took out a flask of water and a container of salt.

Taking up the sword he walked clockwise around the inside of the circle calling out as he did so: "Oh Lord and Spirit of Fire, I call upon thee to guard this circle and witness our rites. Make thou an unbreakable ring that the dark forces shall not cross. I call thee in the Holy Name."

He then performed the same perambulation with the wand, calling on the Spirits of Air. Then, taking the container of salt, he transferred some to the pewter dish and walked around the circle again scattering salt on the ground and appealing to the Spirits of Earth. Finally he poured some water from the flask into the chalice and circulated for the fourth time, sprinkling water around the circle and invoking the Spirits of Water. When he had done all this he replaced the magical implements on the altar and sat down on a low, half-sunken boulder, bidding me do the same.

"Now our barriers are ready," he said, "so we may as well have some refreshment while I explain what our strategy will be if the enemy breaks through them, as he may well do."

This time the airline bag was opened, and out of it North extracted a vacuum flask, from which he poured out two mugs of steaming coffee.

I drank eagerly while North explained our plan for dealing with our attacker.

"Be prepared," he warned me, "for something pretty terrifying. But remember that the outward shape of the being is only an illusion and that the less afraid you are the better chance you stand of resisting it. He held out his hand, and in the palm was a bronze medallion, about three inches in diameter, inscribed with Hebrew letters and strange patterns. "This is the talisman," he said. "Take it and hold on to it until I give the word." I took the object in my right hand and noticed that it felt surprisingly heavy.

"The entity that comes to attack us," North went on, "will go for me first. When I give the order you must throw the talisman at it. That will take it by surprise just when it thinks it has the better of us. Then we will know whether or not we have succeeded." He looked at this watch. "In a few minutes it will be midnight. Any time from then on L.O.Q. could start using his talisman, and I must be ready to block him."

Soon, from down in the valley, came the faint chiming of a church clock, carried on a wind that in the past few minutes had become stronger. By the time the clock had struck twelve North was standing by the altar, sword in hand, eyes closed and an expression of concentration on his face. The wind was now shaking the trees, sending the branches groaning and cracking together; but there was a feeling that its full gust was being held back like an angry dog snarling, straining and snapping at its chain.

Then quite suddenly the wind ceased and the branches of the

trees were still. At the same time I saw that North was making an extra effort of concentration. The muscles of his face were tense. His body swung round as though seeking a magnetic point and came to rest facing westward. He raised the sword and pointed it ahead of him. Then he began a three-syllable chant, in a low, even tone: "Ee-ay-oh, ee-ay-oh, ee-ay-oh..."

The chant continued for what seemed a long time. It could have been five, ten, or twenty minutes – I could not say. But at length my attention was caught by something moving between the trees. At first I thought my eyes were deceiving me when I saw a vague white shape between two of the trunks, for when I turned my head toward it the thing was gone. But it reappeared at another gap, and this time I knew that there was something there. North had seen it too. When he turned and pointed his sword toward it, continuing his chant, the thing moved quickly away and reappeared in another gap. To begin with it was merely a round, white, misty shape with something oddly characteristic about the way it moved. Just as one can sometimes recognize someone when one catches, through the corner of one's eye, a particular way of moving without actually seeing the person, so I apprehended something familiar in the movement of this object. I was soon given the explanation, for the white mass gradually became more clearly defined, and it was the legs that took shape first. They were those of a giant spider. Then gradually three heads began to form. On the left was that of a cat, on the right that of a toad, and in the middle was a human face. It was a thin, emaciated face of such malevolence that I instinctively moved toward North for protection.

"It's worse than I thought," he said in a low voice, breaking off the chant. "That is the demon of the talisman, Bael himself. Stay by me and do as I say."

We watched the creature move several times around the ring of trees. Then it came slowly toward our own circle and halted when it reached the rope. Its black, hairy legs reached upward with strangely delicate movements and seemed to encounter some invisible obstacle. It moved to a different position on the circle and tried again, but still the obstacle was there, as though we were encased in a magical bell-jar. But our protection did not last for long. The thing backed away from the circle then rushed forward again with its scuttling movement and at the last moment leapt into the air. It landed just inside the circle, and the struggle of crossing the barrier seemed to have weakened it, for it swayed and staggered and for a moment seemed to be on the point of collapse. But it recovered its strength and began to advance slowly toward North.

He stood firm, his sword pointing at the creature, and his face showed no trace of fear as the thing came closer. But when it was almost upon him and looked as though it was preparing to envelope him with its legs, he shouted out: "The talisman! Now!"

I had the object ready in my right hand, and at his command I threw it from close range at the spider's body. As it struck its mark the creature gave a squeal of pain and fell back, its legs flailing uncontrollably. For a moment I thought the battle was won, but then the monster pulled itself together and turned to look for its attacker.

Then it was advancing again, this time toward me, its human face fixing me with eyes that glowed with a red luminosity.

I fought in vain against my rising terror, increased by the sight of North who had fallen to the ground from the exhaustion of his struggle and was weakly trying to raise himself up. The thing continued toward me. I backed away and as I did so, tripped over a stone and fell on my back. I raised myself on my elbows to see the creature poised for attack. I closed my eyes, telling myself that it was all an illusion, willing it to vanish, but at any moment I expected to feel the hairy limbs clasping me. Instead, I heard a sound that startled me, a great bellow which resounded through the night air. Simultaneously there came a strong animal smell – an earthy smell that reminded me of farms and stable-yards. Some primal earth-force was present that gave me a sense of protection. The spider creature, however, reacted with terror. When I opened my eyes I saw it stop in its tracks and slowly turn around. Then I saw the source of the bellow. A huge bull was standing on the spot where the talisman had fallen, an animal twice the size of a normal bull and with a vast pair of wings rising from its body. The bull bellowed again, and at the sound the other creature turned and fled from the circle. The bull galloped after it through the trees. For a few moments they were hidden, then through a gap in the trees I saw them in the distance as they disappeared where the land dipped downward. A faint bellow was carried on the breeze and then all was quiet.

North had stood up and was searching for the talisman. He found it lying where it had fallen and, with a sigh of relief, wrapped it in a piece of white silk and put it in his pocket. Then he came and clasped my shoulder with his right hand. "Thank you, Paul," he said. "You've done great work tonight. We shan't see Bael again. Having failed with us he will now turn on the man who sent him, and I wouldn't like to be in the shoes of L.O.Q. now."

We did not speak as we made our way back over the path by which we had come. I guessed that North must be feeling as exhausted as I was, but I did notice that something in the atmosphere, some tension, had disappeared, as though an impending thunderstorm had somehow melted away. We said goodbye when we reached the cars, and I drove back home through the thin light of the early dawn.

As I walked up to the front door of the terraced house I knocked over one of the milk bottles that were waiting to be taken away when the morning delivery arrived. The hollow sound that it made as it rolled over the stone porch jerked me violently back into my everyday self. As I picked up the bottle unbroken and replaced it with the other three in a neat row, I was suddenly aware of how comforting it was to be back in a world where milk was delivered, morning papers and post came and people marched off with rolled umbrellas to their humdrum jobs. The knowledge that I could never again be fully part of that world made me appreciate it all the more.

It was about six in the morning when I let myself into the house. Sally must have heard me because she came into the kitchen in her dressing-gown while I was making an early breakfast. She gave me a kiss then looked me up and down.

"Good heavens, Paul, you look as though you've been up all night, and you've got mud on your clothes. What on earth have you been doing?"

I tried to sound casual. "Oh, we went to a clearing in the woods to do a kind of ritual."

"Really? What kind of ritual?"

I groped for a way to explain to her the strange apparitions I had seen. I was beginning to wonder myself how much of it had been real and how much I had imagined. "Well it was a kind of guided vision. We conjured up certain archetypal images and sent them out into the world to do battle for the forces of light."

She looked at me with an expression of mock severity. "Hah! A harmless experiment you said! Well, after such a mighty battle you must be starving, and I'm pretty famished myself. I'll make some bacon and eggs."

6

I went to see North at Ravenhurst the following Wednesday evening, arriving after dinner as I usually did. The maid showed me into the study where he was standing in front of the fire holding a decanter of port as though he had known I was just about to walk in . He filled two glasses on a side table, and the rich, red liquid captured and held the glow of the log fire. It was not until we had talked for a while about small things and our glasses had been emptied and refilled that North referred to our nocturnal battle of a few days earlier. He asked me to describe everything that had happened on that occasion as I remembered it. I did so, and when I came to the sudden appearance of the bull, he interrupted.

"You are sure it was a bull?" he asked.

"Yes, a bull with wings is how I would have described it."

He nodded. "That confirms my own impression, but one always has to be absolutely sure. It's so easy to project one's imaginings on to any kind of apparition. The point is that this means the talisman we used to combat Bael is something more powerful than I had originally thought, and something more significant, too."

"In what way?"

"Well, what does the bull signify to you in the occult sense?"

I thought for a moment. "The astrological sign Taurus."

"Exactly, but there's more to it than that. Taurus is one of the four zodiacal signs that have a special meaning; the others are Leo, Scorpio, and Aquarius. In the Egyptian zodiac Scorpio is an eagle, and these four symbols of the Bull, the Lion, the Eagle, and the Man carry a profound message. They are the four faces of the Cherub of Ezekiel described in the Old Testament. I'll see if I can find the passage."

He stood up and searched among the bookshelves until he found an old, leather-bound Bible. "Let me see," he flicked through the pages. "Yes, here we are, this is the passage in the King James Version:

'And I looked, and, behold, a whirlwind came out of the north, a great cloud, and a fire infolding itself, and a brightness was about it, and out of the midst thereof as the colour of amber, out of the midst of the fire. Also out of the midst thereof came the likeness of four living creatures. And this was their appearance; they had the likeness of a man. And every one had four faces, and every one had four wings. And their feet were straight feet; and the sole of their feet was like the sole of a calf's foot: and they sparkled like the colour of burnished brass. And they had the hands of a man under their wings on their four sides; and they four had their faces and their wings. Their wings were joined one to another; they turned not when they went; they went every one straight forward. As for the likeness of their faces, they four had the face of a man and the face of a lion on the right side: and they four had the face of an ox on the left side; they four also had the face of an eagle.'"

North stopped reading and put down the book. "In the esoteric tradition," he went on, "the four creatures represent different things. First they represent the elements: the bull is earth, the lion is fire, the eagle is water, and the man is air."

"But surely," I broke in, "the eagle should be air and the man water."

He shook his head. "You'd think it would be that way round, but it isn't. Aquarius, the water-carrier, is not a water but an air sign. And the eagle, which later became Scorpio, is a water sign. The devilish thing about occult correspondences is that they are never cut and dried. In any set of related symbols there's always some anomaly. And this reflects the truth that no doctrine can live without an element of paradox and mystery.

"The four symbols represent four successive ages in the world's development, each standing for a different state of consciousness. First comes the bull of the earth, the primitive urges of survival and procreation that sustain man at his basic level. Then comes the eagle of water and the emotions which brings about a superstructure of religion and art. Next there follows the lion, the driving force of the intellect that gives us science and technology. Finally, in the fourth stage, we have the air of spiritual attainment which incorporates within it all the other elements, just as the basic form of the entire cherub is that of a man. Only in the fourth stage does man really become man and cease to be merely a higher member of the animal kingdom."

"And have we reached the fourth stage yet?" I asked.

"Not the world as a whole, no. Of course all four forces are present in every situation, but only in the fourth do all of them fall into proper balance. It is possible for an individual to attain this balance within himself, but society as a whole is still in the third stage, the stage in which scientific and technological values are dominant. The search for the balanced fourth state has been enshrined in various occult traditions for thousands of years. We see it, for example, in the four suits of the Tarot cards – wands, swords, cups, and pentacles – and in the four objects of the Grail legends – the lance, the sword, the cup, and the stone. In Christian tradition the four archetypal animals were made to represent the four gospels: Mark as the lion, John as the eagle, Luke as the bull, and Matthew as the man. But this fourfold concept can be traced back much farther than even Ezekiel.

"You see legend has it that thousands of years ago, before recorded history, there was a golden age when men knew how to combine all four forces in harmony. There are various theories about where this golden civilization existed. Some people say that it was on a remote island in the north Atlantic called Thule. Other people talk of a place called Atlantis, a continent somewhere in the mid-Atlantic that is supposed to have sunk into the ocean. Another theory – and this is the one I prefer – says that the island which people call Atlantis or Thule was in fact ancient Britain and that the golden age flourished long before the Romans came.

"The thing that is common to all these theories is the belief that fragments of the great wisdom possessed by the vanished race passed into a secret tradition which has been handed down to the present day. But there are those who believe that it was not just the tradition that was handed down. There is a school of thought which says that the fourfold power of the golden civilization was enshrined in four sacred objects and that these passed down through a succession of guardians. At the break-up of the golden age the four objects – let us call them the Tetrad for convenience – were separated and dispersed to different parts of the world. But it is said that one day they will be brought back together again and that the nation which re-unites them will have the power to resurrect the golden age.

"The knowledge of the Tetrad has passed into the collective memory of the human race, and every culture has produced its own symbolic version of it. Even modern psychology has reproduced this fourfold pattern. Carl Jung speaks of four modes of thinking: observation, intuition, reason, and feeling. He knew that the Tetrad exists both in the cosmos and in man himself. William Blake realized the same thing when he spoke of the "four mighty ones" in every man.

"But few people have had more than a dim knowledge of the existence of the real, physical Tetrad. One who did was Eliphas Lévi, and he writes in his *Doctrine and Ritual of High Magic* that the destiny of humanity is being contested by the princes of the world's four quarters, and that the leadership of humanity will go to the nation that holds the Keys of the East. His reference to the Keys of the East shows that he knew all about the Tetrad. The east is the realm of air, the master element in the Tetrad and the symbol of the final stage.

"Lévi at first believed that France was to be the country that would lead the world into a new golden age, but in the last few months of his life he came to the conclusion that he was wrong and that Britain was to play this role. This is why he gave the Talisman of Althotas to Hadley's teacher. You see I am convinced that the talisman is in fact the original pentacle of the Tetrad and that Lévi knew this. If so, then he must have tried to find out where the other three members were, but nowhere in his writing does he seem to give any clue."

"Could it be," I suggested, "that his clues were written in some kind of code?"

"More than likely," North nodded, "but the question is, how do we begin to find the cipher?"

An idea suddenly occurred to me. I had a friend who had worked in intelligence during the war and was an expert on ciphers. He also happened to be interested in the occult tradition. When I told North about this man he was immediately interested, and suggested that I go and see him and ask if he could help. I left with a promise that I would do this as soon as possible.

As it happened, however, something else intervened before I could contact my friend. A few weeks earlier I had published a short article on Eliphas Lévi in a small occult journal called *Athanor*, and the very morning after my conversation with North I received a letter, written in blue ink in a sprawling, continental hand, from an address in Islington. It read:

"Dear. Mr. Cairns,

In view of your recent article on Eliphas Lévi in *Athanor* I am wondering whether you might be interested in seeing, and possibly acquiring, some documents connected with Lévi which are in my possession. If you wish to see them perhaps you would care to ring me and arrange a time.

Yours sincerely,

........"

The signature was indecipherable. It looked like "Hugo" something.

Later that day I rang the number given, and a quiet, slightly drawling voice with a Germanic accent answered. Its owner introduced himself as Hugo von Falkendorf. I explained who I was, and he invited me to come round the following afternoon to look at his documents. I asked if I could bring North with me, and he agreed.

As I suspected, North was eager to come when I told him about this development, and at five o'clock the following afternoon we found ourselves ringing the doorbell of a house in a quiet Georgian street near the Angel. It was one of those doors with an entry phone so that the occupants of the house could check their visitors before letting them in. We said who we were, and the door opened with a slight buzz.

We mounted two flights of stairs to the top of the house. Waiting at the open door of the top flat was a thin, dark-haired man who looked slightly too old for the faded denim suit that he was wearing. He held himself with a slight hunch of the shoulders, and when we came up he shook hands with each of us in turn. As he did so he smiled, and I saw that his teeth bore the blackened signs of much smoking.

"Do come in," he said in a quiet, courteous voice, and ushered us into what appeared to be the main room of the flat, a big room overlooking the Regent's Canal. It was one of the most untidy apartments I have ever seen. Clearly its occupant was an artist of some kind, for there were paintings in various states of completion stacked around the walls and standing on easels. The smell of paint, turpentine and other artist's materials hung in the air, mingled with the rancid odor of cigarette smoke. A big, square table by one of the two windows was covered with palettes, tubes of paint and bits of brightly-stained rag as well as an ashtray brimming with cigarette stubs. The only incongruous note was struck by a portrait in a gilt frame over the mantlepiece. It appeared to be of about 18th-century date and showed a man in a wig wearing a blue coat. Across his chest was slung a sash, and from his neck hung a masonic square and compass pendant. This portrait contrasted oddly with the other paintings in the room which were aggressively abstract in style.

Our host cleared a pile of books and a small black cat from a battered-looking sofa with a chintz cover in the middle of the room and invited us to sit down. Then he lit up a cigarette.

"You must excuse the disorder," he said. "The fact is that I am not going to be living here for very much longer, so I have been postponing tidying the place up until I leave. I suppose you could call me the typical disorganized artist. However, I can offer you some tea if you would like." He gestured toward a low wooden cupboard on top of which was a teapot with a cracked lid, a kettle, a packet of tea, a bag of sugar, and some cups and saucers. We accepted, and he set about filing the kettle from a sink and plugging it in. Then he began to pace with a rather cat-like movement up and down the room while he waited for the kettle to boil.

"Before I show you the material," he said, "it might be helpful to you to know a bit about its provenance. The fact is that you see before you the scion of one of the great families of the Habsburg Empire. Over there..." he pointed to the portrait "...is my great-great-grandfather, Count Friedrich von Falkendorf."

Suddenly I could see a likeness – the same thin, beaked nose and slightly harsh mouth, the same deeply set, dark eyes.

"He was a general in the Austrian army and was also a leading Freemason and a practitioner of alchemy. He had a laboratory in his castle, Vogelstein, on the Danube."

As he spoke, I saw that our host had some kind of nervous condition which every now and then made the right-hand corner of his mouth give a rapid series of little twitches. The effect was slightly disconcerting.

"The grand-daughter of this man," he went on, "was my grandmother, Olga von Falkendorf, a remarkable woman with a very deep knowledge of occultism – these things ran in the family. She received part of her education in Paris and while there, through her occult interests, met a young Frenchman, François de Carnac. They were both disciples of Eliphas Lévi for a time. They married in 1872 and for some reason moved back to Austria to live in Vienna. Meanwhile he continued to correspond with Lévi and made occasional trips back to Paris to see him until, near the end of Lévi's life, they fell out, and all contact ceased. Then, about five years after his marriage he also had some deep disagreement with his wife, and they split up, but not before they had produced a child. That was my father, Arthur, who took his mother's name.

"Now we come to a strange part of the story. De Carnac went to live separately in Vienna, and never saw his wife and child. Then, on the eve of a trip he was about to make to France, his manservant found him dead in his bedroom from no apparent cause. There is more to this than meets the eye, as you will see when you read the papers I am going to show you. Some of these consist of various diaries, notebooks, and manuscripts belonging to my grandmother. The rest are diaries kept by de Carnac and handed over to his wife after his death. Both sets of papers were inherited by my father when the old lady died in 1942. By that time he and my mother and myself had taken refuge in England."

"But not your grandmother," North interrupted, "she didn't come with you to England?"

"No, she was too stubborn for that. Just before the Nazis marched into Austria in 1938 my father decided to leave. He did everything in his power to persuade grandmother to come, but she refused point blank. By that time she was living at Schloss Vogelstein – all alone except for a married couple who acted as housekeeper and handyman. So we left her to fend for herself and came to England. From the letters we got from her we gathered that she was living perfectly happily and unmolested. Then in 1942 we heard that she had died, and soon afterward we received a mysterious parcel from Switzerland containing all her most important papers. We never found out who sent it, but whoever it was must have had considerable difficulty in smuggling the papers out of the Reich."

Von Falkendorf stopped to fill the teapot and then pour out three cups. After handing us our cups he squatted cross-legged near the gas fire, holding his teacup with both hands as though to draw warmth from it.

"Well, after the war was over," he continued, "we went back to Austria, and my parents picked up as much of their old life as they could. We had a house in Grinzing, and my father got a teaching post in anthropology at the university. By then Schloss Vogelstein was a ruin. The Russians had bombarded it to pieces. However, we did discover that the housekeeper and her husband had survived and were living in Klosterneuburg. We visited her there one day, and she told us that grandmother had lived peacefully and quietly until her death. Only once had she been bothered by the authorities. The Nazis, as you may know, were suspicious of occultism – that is anything that was not their own brand of occultism. Well, not surprisingly they heard about my grandmother and decided to investigate her.

"One morning the housekeeper was sweeping the hall when she looked out of the window and saw a black car coming up the drive. It stopped in front of the house and two men, unmistakably from the Gestapo, got out. The housekeeper ran quickly upstairs to warn my grandmother who was having breakfast in bed. She told the housekeeper not to worry and just to let the two men in and show them up to the bedroom. The housekeeper went down again, by which time the Gestapo men were pounding on the door and shouting to be let in. She opened the door and showed them upstairs. Then she went down and started to sweep the floor again. A few minutes later she heard from upstairs the noise of the bedroom door being thrown violently open. Then the two men came rushing downstairs, their faces ashen. They flew out of the front door and tumbled into their car, and she watched them drive away at high speed.

"Thinking that something terrible must have happened to grandmother, the housekeeper went upstairs again to find the old lady sitting up in bed calmly sipping her coffee. When asked what had happened, she just said: 'Oh nothing, I only showed them something.'"

"So what was it that she showed them?" I asked.

"Well," our host went on "I have to explain that Olga's fraternity possessed a substance called the Elixir of Concentrated Energy, a powerful alchemical preparation that could be used for healing and promoting longevity. But also, if you exposed a few drops to the air and breathed the vapour, you would experience powerful visions that would represent your darkest fears. These visions would appear like figures in a greenish mist. Now the housekeeper reported that there was a curious, pungent smell in the room and a remnant of greenish vapour, so I believe that my grandmother used the Elixir to scare the wits out of the two Gestapo men. Certainly they never bothered her again. However, I am digressing. I must show you the papers."

He opened the cupboard on which the tea things were standing and pulled out a large cardboard box which he dumped on the sofa between us. North and I spent the next half hour making a quick survey of its contents. In addition to the two sets of diaries there were a number of notebooks filled with notes on alchemy, Kabbalah and the Tarot. Then there were some other manuscripts in different hands. One in particular stood out. It was a folio volume, bound in pigskin, and was written in a neat German Gothic hand, interspersed with many illustrations, some coloured, of alchemical symbols and laboratory processes. It was dated 1763, and the title was the curious mixture of German and Latin often found in documents of that type: *Thesaurus der hochlöblichen Brüderschaft des Rosenkreuzes* (The Treasure House of the Most Praiseworthy Rosicrucian Brotherhood).

"I thought that one would catch your eye," said von Falkenberg when he saw North leafing through the manuscript. "It's one of the Rosicrucian books of instruction that were circulated secretly among the brotherhood. There is, to my knowledge, only one other copy of that one, in the Austrian National Library in Vienna."

As North turned the pages I looked over his shoulder. I could make little of the strange illustrations: the crow devouring the entrails of a corpse, the dragon with its tail in its mouth, the hermaphrodite figure with the heads of a man and a woman, the lion eating the sun. It was like some unfamiliar hieroglyphic language. I could not decipher it, but I could sense that it held an important message. Half way through North paused at a page showing a drawing of a sword, held upright by hand emerging from a cloud, the upper part of the blade encircled by a crown from which hung two leafy branches. A stylised rose marked the centre of the cross-piece, where the handle joined the blade. In the background was the skyline of a city and, further away, a range of hills. Underneath the picture was some writing in a spidery Gothic hand that was almost illegible.

North closed the volume, put it back with the other documents and patted the bulky box. "How much do you want for all this stuff?" he asked.

Von Falkenberg's mouth twitched at the corner, and he drew deeply at his cigarette before saying thoughtfully: "Well, I don't think I could part with it for less than three hundred pounds."

"Agreed," North said without hesitation. "Three hundred it is."

If von Falkenberg was surprised by North's immediate acceptance of his figure he did not show it. He nodded quietly and watched while North wrote out a cheque. I thought that he might insist on clearing the cheque before he parted with his documents, but he evidently trusted North, and a few minutes later we were in a taxi taking the box of papers back to North's flat. We had an early dinner at a nearby Italian restaurant and then returned to the flat to spend the evening studying our acquisition.

7

As soon as I began to study the material properly I saw why North had so readily paid three hundred pounds for it. I also realized what an extraordinary coincidence it was that the documents should come into our hands at this precise moment, for they contained some of the information for which North had searched in vain in Lévi's writings. They also left some questions tantalizingly unanswered. But what mainly held my attention was the story which emerged from them and which can best be retold by quoting from the two sets of diaries. First, some extracts from those of François de Carnac.

23 April, 1872

Returned to Paris today from Bordeaux to take up my legal studies. The prospect fills me with boredom, but I suppose I shall have to see it through for the sake of my father's memory – not to mention the money I shall get under the terms of his will when I qualify. I have taken a room near the Opera, on the top floor with quite a pleasant view toward Montmartre.

30 April

I am bored to distraction already by my studies, and this wretched city offers no light relief – all the spark seems to have gone out of it since the war with Prussia and then the accursed communards. God knows how I am going to endure several more years of it.

2 May

A curious encounter today. I was passing a little bookshop near the Seine and went in to see if I could find something to read that would alleviate the tedium of my existence. There were several novels by Balzac on one of the shelves, and I picked out *La Peau de Chagrin* and started to dip into it. In a short while I was intrigued – a strange story of a magic ass's skin which shrinks every time it grants a wish and will one day shrink away altogether signalling the end of its owner's life. As I stood reading I became aware of somebody standing near me. I turned to see an old man with a bald head fringed with long white hair, dressed in a kind of priest's robe and holding a stick with an unusual ivory handle carved into a curling shape. My eyes met his for a moment. They were a pale shade of blue, very clear and penetrating. At that moment the shopkeeper came up, so I paid for the book and left the shop. The old man left at the same time, and as we emerged into the street he said:

"Excuse me, Sir, I couldn't help noticing what you were reading. It's a most remarkable book. May I ask if you have a special interest in the esoteric side of Balzac's work?"

I said no and that I had only bought the book to alleviate my boredom.

"And what is the cause of this boredom?" he asked.

"Not one that you could remove, I'm afraid, Father," I replied, assuming him to be a priest.

"You are mistaken," he said with a slight smile, "I am not a priest. May I introduce myself. My name is Eliphas Lévi."

"Ah, you are a rabbi then."

He shook his head. "No, I bear a Hebrew name, but I am not of the Jewish race."

"You are a mysterious fellow," I laughed. "If you are neither a priest nor a rabbi then what are you?"

"A student of the Highest Science," he replied gravely.

"And what science might that be?"

In answer the old man handed me an address card. It bore his name and what I assumed to be its equivalent in Hebrew letters underneath. The address was 155 Rue de Sèvres. "Your question," he said, "cannot be answered in a few words, but if you wish to talk with me at length then please feel free to call on me. I am usually at home in the evenings." With that he bowed slightly and was gone.

I put the card in my pocket and forgot all about it until later that evening when I happened to be chatting on the stairs to Monsieur Bailleul, the brisk little civil servant who lives on the floor below. He asked me what the book was that I was holding under my arm, and that reminded me of the bookshop and my meeting with the old man. I showed Bailleul the card, and he immediately exclaimed: "But my dear fellow, haven't you heard of this man? He's quite a celebrity. Two or three times he's been put in prison as a political agitator, but he's best known for his books on magical subjects. I've looked at them and found them a bit beyond me, but by all accounts he's an interesting fellow. I should call on him if you've been invited."

What Bailleul told me has made me curious to see the old man again. I think I shall take up his invitation.

6 May

I believe this to have been a decisive day in my life. I have just returned from visiting M. Lévi and must record what I can remember of the evening – in any case I am too excited to sleep.

Just before 7 o'clock I went to the address in the Rue de Sèvres. I climbed the stairs to the second floor and found myself in front of a door to which was pinned a card on which some characters which I recognized from the visiting card as the name Eliphas Lévi in Hebrew. The letters were written alternately in red, yellow and blue. In black, in the corners of the card, were the four letters I.N.R.I.

I knocked at the door, and a moment later it was opened by my host, dressed in the same type of robe as before. He invited me into a pleasant room overlooking some gardens and filled with books. On the walls hung a curious assortment of portraits: Rabelais, Voltaire, Rousseau and Saint Sophia. But the most remarkable thing of all was a metal object which stood by itself on a small round table and looked like some kind of complicated astronomical instrument. From a base like that of a candlestick rose a series of branches to which were attached a bewildering array of spheres, dials and triangular shapes.

When I asked Monsieur Lévi what this object was he replied that it was a device for predicting events. "It was invented," he said, "by one of the noblest, most brilliant and least recognized minds of the century." He went on to describe the inventor as a Polish expatriate mathematician and occultist who had incorporated in his machine all the basic mathematical laws that govern the cosmos and human events. It was called a "prognometer."

"Can you give me a demonstration of its power?" I asked.

"Certainly," replied Lévi. Tell me that day, month and year of your birth, and your full name."

I told him these details, and he made some quick calculation on a piece of paper. Then he applied himself to the machine, turning dials and adjusting the positions of spheres until he evidently had the results he wanted. Then, still looking at the machine, he said: "Your father died when you were ten years old. At fourteen you had a serious illness from which you nearly died. Since adolescence you have nurtured a burning ambition to be a poet which outside pressures have so far prevented you from fulfilling..."

I held up my hand. "Enough," I said. "You have already astounded me. How could you possibly know all this?"

"In the cosmos," he replied, "everything is related to everything else, from the falling of a single leaf to the overthrow of a civilization. This machine is a model of the cosmos. I merely use the machine to proceed from the data you gave me to the other things I told you. I could equally well have told you that King Louis-Philippe lost his throne because he carried an umbrella or that Frederick the Great's predilection for grilled mushrooms saved him from defeat in the Seven Years' War."

"But does this mean," I asked, "that my life is mapped out before me and that there is nothing I can do to change its course?"

He shook his head. "Many possible routes are open to you. It's up to you to choose which one you wish to follow."

"So there is still free will?"

"Yes. Will is like the magic ass's skin in that story by Balzac that you were reading when we met. You remember how the hero, de

Valentin, is on the point of suicide when he suddenly comes into possession of the skin? Well the skin stands for human will and signifies that there is nothing a human being cannot achieve provided he is willing to make the necessary sacrifice in terms of the stock of will power available to him. Our will power is greatest when we are willing to sacrifice everything we posses, including life itself. The wise man reserves his sacrifices for the things that really matter, then he sacrifices willingly and joyfully. Valentin's tragedy is that he comes to realize the immense power he possesses, but is unable to use it wisely. First he spends it profligately on luxurious living, then hoards it jealously. In the end he spends it carelessly in spite of himself and dies having failed to use his power for anything really important. The science of magic teaches man to use his will to bring about changes in himself and the world. The true magician has the power that comes from knowing what task he wishes to perform and being able to pour his entire will into it. Such a man, armed with the knowledge which a machine like this can give..." he put his hand on the apparatus he had just demonstrated "...could be a force to reckon with in the world."

"And what," I asked, "does the machine tell you about the future of mankind?"

"It confirms what has already been written down in the secret traditions," he replied and began to tell me about four phases in the history of civilization and how we were approaching the fourth phase when one nation would emerge to lead the world into a new golden age. He said this age would begin when four objects of a powerful Tetrad were re-assembled. The four objects correspond to those of the Tarot: the wand, the sword, the cup and the pentacle. He showed me a talisman he possesses which he believes to be the original pentacle. He calls it the Talisman of Althotas. He is convinced that the other objects will be brought together here in France and that the French nation will usher in the new golden age.

We talked far into the night, and when I finally returned home my head was spinning with the massive implications of all that I had been told. I must think deeply about all this before I pay my next visit. Already I feel a strange exhilaration, as though I had awakened to the realization of a new force within me.

14 July

I have been seeing the Master regularly now for some time. I have joined a small circle of about eight pupils that meets at his apartment once a week. The other members are a curious mixture of types and nationalities. There is an expatriate Russian nobleman, a middle-aged Englishwoman and a rather nervous Italian who delivers long monologues while twitching a little goatee beard. There are also a number of French people who come and go, mostly quite respectable types—civil servants, lawyers, teachers. The Master has the gift of being able to reach each one of them on his own level and make each feel his own worth as an individual. I feel as though a whole new world had opened up for me. I now know that my destiny lies in helping the Master to bring about the New Golden Age. My poetic ambitions pale before such a mighty task.

22 July

A new member has joined the group – a young Austrian girl. Her name is Olga von Falkendorf. She is small and dark with blue eyes and has an extraordinary, quiet force – like still fire.

3 September

Olga went back to Austria for the month of August, but is more in my thoughts than ever. She should be back again at the next meeting. I wonder if I shall have the courage to declare my feelings for her."

This entry came at the end of a volume, and the next volume in chronological order began several years later. Some of the intervening period, however, was filled in by Olga's diaries, which sketched in briefly her courtship with de Carnac, their marriage, and their setting up house in Vienna. The tone of her account showed that her attitude to François was protective, if not to say maternal. She seemed to regard herself as having a mission to provide a stabilizing element in his life that would enable him to bring his gifts to fruition. It was also clear that she did not hero-worship Lévi to the same extent as he did.

Very soon after their marriage she began to indicate that all was not well. There were hints that she had joined a fraternity of some kind without her husband's knowledge, and one entry read: "François is not yet ready to be introduced. He still persists in his slavish devotion to Lévi, and this absurd conviction that the Tetrad is to be re-assembled in France. He does not and must not know that one of the four is in our keeping."

A few weeks later she wrote: "François has returned from France in a state of shock. Lévi evidently no longer pins his hopes on France as the saviour of civilization. He now believes that England will play the role and has given his pentacle and the prognometer to an English disciple. François feels betrayed, but perhaps he will see things in a clearer perspective now."

But her hope was not fulfilled. François became withdrawn and morose, and she began to suspect that he was becoming involved with an opposing fraternity to whom she simply referred to as "them". She tried to warn him against the dangers of this involvement, but without success. "Whenever I raise the subject he just tells me to mind my own business." Soon after this Lévi died, and she recorded that François refused even to attend the funeral. After this their relationship became steadily worse, and finally came the entry: "François has moved to a house in another part of Vienna. There is nothing more I can do. He has made his bed. Now he must lie on it."

The story was taken up again by François's diary. In the autumn of 1876, after he had left his wife, he recorded: "I was a fool to be taken in by Lévi's chauvinistic talk. The power of the Tetrad belongs with those who know how to use it. My new masters have taught me that. They alone have the courage and the vision to deserve the power. At the moment they have none of the Four, but I may be able to help them. I think I know where the sword is. Olga believed that I knew nothing of her fraternity, but I am more perceptive than she thinks. I believe I can penetrate their stronghold."

Two days later he wrote: "At last I know where the vault is. Tonight I shall take possession of the sword and then go to Paris with it to await further instructions."

This was the last entry he ever made. The story was completed by Olga's diary: "A terrible tragedy has happened. François tried last night to enter the vault and was killed by the barriers guarding it. I blame myself, for I must have somehow given him a clue to the position of the vault. I feel the deepest of grief, even though he brought it upon himself. His body was returned secretly to his apartment so that the authorities do not try to find out what he was doing at the time of his death."

8

It was nearly eleven o'clock by the time we had finished reading the diaries. We put them down with a feeling of mingled excitement and frustration. North was now sure that the sword described by de Carnac was the one he was looking for – the sword of the Tetrad. And he also suspected that it was the same one as depicted in the alchemical manuscript, which he now opened again at the page showing the sword. Taking a Tarot pack from a drawer, he extracted the ace of swords and laid it beside the drawing.

"You see," he said "most of the details are the same – the hand coming out of the cloud, the crown, the branches. And look at the city in the background. Do you recognise it?"

I peered at the drawing. One feature that stood out was a large medieval church or cathedral in the centre. It had a high, pitched roof and a very tall spire, tacked oddly on to the south side of the nave. "I believe it's Vienna," I said. "That looks like St. Stephen's Cathedral. And those wooded hills in the background must be the Vienna Woods."

"That would make sense," North said. "in the light of de Carnac's diary. And von Falkendorf mentioned that the only other copy of the manuscript is in Vienna. Can you read the writing underneath?"

I asked for a magnifying glass. He brought one and I spent several minutes trying to decipher the writing. It began: "The sword commands the powers of the East and of Air. It is encircled by a crown, signifying that it is destined for a king or a great leader who shall banish the forces of evil and usher in the Golden Age. In the meantime the sword rests in an imperial city, concealed in ..." The rest of the writing was indistinct and in places the ink was faded. Deciphering it would be a slow and painstaking task.

North suggested that I take the manuscript home with me to work on at my leisure and see if I could read enough of the inscription to find out where in Vienna the sword was located. He warned me to take care of the volume, but, with that strangely casual practicality of his, gave me a brown paper carrier bag from the kitchen for me to take it home in.

Having left the flat I made my way to Lancaster Gate tube station with three quarters of an hour to get to Euston and catch my last train home. In the underground train I could not resist getting the book out to have another look at those strange pictures. Just after we had passed Bond Street station I was vaguely aware of a shabbily-dressed, unshaven man who came lurching past me smelling of beer and sweat and flopped into the seat beside me. The only other people in the carriage were a group of half a dozen American tourists and a Salvation Army couple – all of them down at the far end of the carriage.

Suddenly, without any warning, the sleeve of a greasy raincoat was thrust across the page I was looking at, and a grubby hand snatched away the book.

"Do you mind if I have a look?" said the tramp in an Irish accent. "I always appreciate a good book – being a bit of a scholar myself you understand."

I was panic-stricken at the sight of the priceless volume being flicked through like a railway timetable by the Irishman's dirty fingers. But I was afraid to try and grab the book away for fear of damaging it.

"All right," I said, "but please be careful."

"Be careful," he repeated. "It's valuable then, is it?"

"Yes," I said, "It's valuable," and immediately realized the foolishness of the remark.

As the train drew into Oxford Circus station I made an attempt to take the book back, but he pulled it away and held it almost up to his nose, peering at the page and muttering. I decided to take my time and if necessary travel to the end of the Central Line to get it back.

The doors of the train opened for the Oxford Circus platform, and the tramp continued to peer at the book. Then, taking me completely by surprise, he leapt up and dashed toward the nearest door holding the book. He must have timed it carefully, for the door was closing just as I reached him. I made a grab for his raincoat in an attempt to hold him, but in vain; the belt came away in my hands, and the door closed, trapping me in the carriage. As the train pulled out I could see the thief making for the exit.

There was nothing I could do except report the matter to the police, but there was no point in doing that until the following day. So I made my way miserably home, full of self-recrimination at having been so careless. When I had stopped cursing myself I began to wonder how I could make amends to North, and it occurred to me that there might just be another copy of the manuscript which I could get hold of. If anyone would know how to obtain such a manuscript it would be the occult bookseller Arthur Jenkins whose customer and acquaintance I had been for years.

The next day, therefore, I went to Jenkins' bookshop in Convent Garden and was shown into the little office at the back. Mr. Jenkins rubbed his chin when I told him the title of the manuscript I was seeking, *The Secret Treasure House of the Rosicrucian Brotherhood.*

"I'm afraid I can't hold out much hope for you," he said shaking his head, "but I'll ask around and see if there's any chance of getting a copy. Come back in about a week and I'll tell you if I've had any luck."

He gave me a cup of coffee, and I went away feeling slightly consoled. When I came back a week later he greeted me with a worried look on his face and once again took me into the room at the back of the shop. "I'm afraid I haven't been able to find the manuscript you are looking for, but in the process of searching for it I have discovered something rather puzzling. Within the past month about a dozen alchemical and Rosicrucian manuscripts have disappeared from private collections all over the country. The other dealers I have talked to have been approached by the owners and asked to be on the look-out for them. It can't be coincidence. Whoever the thief is he has some special interest in the Rosicrucians."

I thanked Mr. Jenkins for his trouble and left the shop feeling that the time had come for me to tell North about the situation. When I told him he was less concerned about the loss of his manuscript than about Jenkins' news. "If we knew who the thief was," he said, "we could find out how serious this is. He could be a harmless crank, or he could be something else entirely. What we need is some object connected with him that we could use to identify him clairvoyantly."

I suddenly remembered the belt from the tramp's raincoat, which I had kept in my coat pocket thinking that it might provide a clue. North asked me to bring it, and when I had done so he laid it out on a table and fished a dowser's pendulum out of his pocket—a small ivory weight on the end of a thread. He held this over the belt, and immediately the pendulum began to gyrate in an anti-clockwise direction. Then he held his left hand, palm downward, between the pendulum and the belt. The pendulum stopped and began to gyrate violently in the opposite direction.

"Just as I thought," said North, putting away the pendulum. "The belt shows a violent adverse reaction to me. That means that whoever owns it is my enemy, and that almost certainly points to the fact that the thief is working for L.O.Q. He must be looking for something in those manuscripts – perhaps the sword, perhaps other things as well. What I would like you to do is to find out if any copies of the stolen manuscripts exist and if so where. If we can get hold of any we may be able to find out if indeed the sword is in Vienna and, if so, precisely where it is hidden."

Finding out the titles of the missing manuscripts was not a difficult task. From Arthur Jenkins I obtained the names of the dealers who had been asked to be on the look-out for them and made a list of the titles. Then I consulted various bibliographies and library catalogs. From these I gathered that all of the manuscripts were believed to be unique, except for North's document, *The Secret Treasure House*, one copy of which, as we knew, was in the Austrian National Library in Vienna. North decided immediately that I should go to Vienna at once at his expense and make a thorough study of the document. He said that we could not even afford to waste time in ordering a microfilm, as every day L.O.Q. might be getting nearer to what he was seeking, and if he found it the consequences could be disastrous.

Luckily I was able to arrange a few days' holiday at short notice, and the following day I found myself on a plane to Vienna. I arrived in the early afternoon and went to a pension recommended to me by North, in a quiet street off the Landstrasser Hauptstrasse. It was on the first floor of a rather sombre building with a marble staircase and an ornate cast-iron lift shaft. The pension was run by Frau Schneider, a widow who had once been an actress in the Burgtheater, and the dark mahogany walls of the enormous corridors and rooms were brightened here and there by theater posters and photographs of groups of actors and actresses in costume. The place was both friendly and discreet, as North had said it would be.

I started to unpack. Somewhere below my huge room, with its

heavy wardrobe and tiled stove, a piano was being played – something a little sentimental, Schubert perhaps. At four o'clock Frau Schneider brought me some tea and poppy cake. Then I went for a walk across the river to the Prater and on the way back had supper in a pleasant little Gasthof.

The following morning I went to the manuscript collection of the National Library and asked for the *Secret Treasure House*. When it was brought to me the librarian remarked that someone else had just recently been looking at it. I enquired who the person was and was told that it was a Fräulein Helga Weiss, who lived in the Schüttelstrasse. I made a note of the address and then settled down to study the manuscript.

I quickly found the drawing of the sword, but this time there was no inscription underneath it, so I began to read through the rest of the manuscript. The text described a number of alchemical formulae for different purposes. One was for producing gold, another for making an elixir capable of conferring long life, yet another for mixing an aphrodisiac. Toward the end of the manuscript was a formula rather more cryptic than the rest, the aim of which was to produce "a substance containing concentrated energy which can be released either slowly or suddenly as desired." The key ingredient in the process was not revealed, but I immediately recognised the elixir of concentrated energy that Hugo von Falkendorf had told us about. In another passage there was a reference to the "sword of power" which operated in the spiritual realm as the elixir of concentrated energy operated in the physical.

Both sword and elixir were said to be "in the safe-keeping of the Rosicrucian Fraternity."

After puzzling over the manuscript for a couple of hours I went to have a snack in the library cafe and afterward went into a telephone booth in the entrance hall and looked up the number of Helga Weiss. I dialed it, and after a short pause a female voice with a strong Viennese accent answered. After establishing that the voice belonged to Fräulein Weiss I explained who I was and how I had found out about her.

"I see," she said after a short silence. "Well, we had better have a talk. I suggest that we meet for tea tomorrow afternoon. Do you know the Cafe Zimmerman?"

I said no.

"It's in the Weihburggasse, off the Kärntnerstrasse. I'll see you there at four o'clock."

"How will I know you?"

"Don't worry, I shall know you."

When I returned to the reading room after lunch the manuscript was not on the table where I had left it. A middle-aged woman librarian who had attended to me earlier came over wearing an apologetic expression. "I am very sorry, Herr Cairns," she said, "but the manuscript you were reading is not in fact for public examination. I was not aware of this when I gave it to you, but the head of this department, Dr. Krassny, saw it on the table and said that it would have to be put away again."

I controlled my annoyance and said that perhaps I had better have a word with Dr. Krassny. "Very well," said the woman, "Dr. Krassny is sitting at the desk at the far end of the room."

I observed that Dr. Krassny was also a woman, younger than her colleague and cast in the mould of the Germanic blue-stocking – a thin, rather severe-looking woman with gold-rimmed glasses and fair hair swept back into a bun. Her desk was on a platform, like that of an examination invigilator, so that her head was on a level with mine. She looked up as I approached and, guessing my mission, said:

"Ah, you are Herr Cairns, I presume. I am sorry there was a misunderstanding about the manuscript. You see it happens to belong to a collection given to the library by Professor Irtenkauf, the retired Professor of Archaeology. He called me yesterday and said that he wished this particular manuscript to be withheld from the public unless he gave express permission for it to be seen."

"I see. Does the Professor live in Vienna?"

"Yes."

"Then could you tell me how I can contact him?"

Dr. Krassny hesitated for a moment before replying: "If you are intending to ask his permission I don't think you will succeed, but I'll tell you what. I'll ring up and ask him. He knows me, and I might be able to persuade him."

She picked up the telephone on her desk and dialed. A few moments later I heard her say: "Hello, Professor? This is Dr. Krassny. It's about your manuscript, the *Treasure House of the Rosicrucian Brotherhood*. There's a young man from England here who wants to look at it. Do you think he might have your permission?...Yes I know your instructions, but he seems a respectable person, and I am sure...I see. Very well, then, we must abide by your wishes. Goodbye." She shook her head as she put the receiver down. "I'm sorry. The Professor is quite adamant. He does not wish the manuscript to be consulted."

I was beginning to lose my patience. "But this is preposterous. I have come all the way from England to look at this manuscript, and now you say I can't see it."

"It's not my decision, but the Professor's."

"Well, I that case I think I had better go and see him personally." I was conscious that my anger had made me indiscreet. I should not have revealed that I had made the journey from England specially to see the manuscript.

"Well, you can try," said Dr. Krassny, "but I don't think you'll change his mind. However, here is where he lives." She scribbled an address on a piece of paper and handed it to me. As I left the room I turned and saw her picking up the telephone again.

I walked out into the Heldenplatz and found a taxi to take me to the Professor's address in Heiligenstadt, a suburb near the Danube where Beethoven used to spend his summers. I half expected the brass plaque by the door of the tall, narrow grey-stone house to say that Beethoven had written a symphony there, but it simply bore the name: "Prof. Dr. Karl Irtenkauf". I paid the taxi driver, then walked up to the door. It was of heavy mahogany and had a glass panel covered with a wrought-iron grille. I pulled a handle beside the door, and somewhere inside the house a bell clanged. I waited for what seemed a long time then rang again. Another long wait, then I heard shuffling footsteps approaching the door. It opened a few inches, and an old, grey-haired woman peered through the crack without saying anything.

"Good day," I said. "I wonder if Professor Irtenkauf is at home."

"Who shall I say it is?" said the woman in a flat voice.

"My name is Cairns," I said, "from England."

A flicker of interest passed across her face when I said "England", and she opened the door for me. I found myself in a high-ceilinged hallway of extraordinary gloom. The walls were of dark wood, possibly painted brown, but it was difficult to tell since the only light came from a window just visible at the turn of the heavy carved stairway which ascended form the far end of the hall. The old woman opened a doorway on the left. "Would you wait in here please? I'll tell Herr Professor you are here."

The room into which she showed me was a living room of exactly the kind that one would expect of find in the house of a conservative, respectable Austrian academic. There were many bookshelves around the walls, and in one corner was the inevitable stove, in this case built of dark green tiles. In the opposite corner, near the window, was a grand piano. The furniture was heavy and solid – a big chaise-longue with a carved mahogany back, upholstered in red velvet, several chairs of the same materials, and, by the window, a table on which stood a plaster bust of an Egyptian pharaoh and some photographs in frames. One of them showed a rather attractive woman sitting in a garden holding a boy about three years old. I wondered if it might have been an old photograph of the Frau Professor and her son. If so, I guessed that the Professor was now a widower. The room had a slight shabbiness and untidiness which a house-proud Austrian wife would not have allowed but which clearly did not bother the old housekeeper or her employer.

I had no time to examine the other photographs, for I heard the door opening at the other side of the hall, and then a man's footsteps on the parquet floor. The door of the room opened and a tall, elderly man entered the room. He had a large, round face and two tufts of grey hair flanking a bald forehead. He wore a pair of thick-lensed glasses so that it was difficult to see the colour or expression of his eyes. He came forward carrying himself with a stoop which somehow accentuated his considerable height and bulk.

"How do you do?" he said, shaking my hand. "You are the young man that Dr. Krassny rang about earlier?"

I nodded. "That's right. I came to see you so that I could explain my reasons for wanting to see the manuscript."

"Please sit down," he said, waving toward the chaise-longue. He seated himself in one of the chairs and reached into his pocket for a packet of cigars. He offered one to me, which I refused, then lit one up himself, a long, thin, black cigar with a pungent smell that made me think of the Balkans and of hubble-bubble pipes in a Bosnian bazaar.

I did not feel that I wanted to take him entirely into my confidence, but I told him about the missing copy of the manuscript and made up a story that I was engaged in research into alchemy and needed to read this particular document. When I had finished he sat puffing at his cigar for a few minutes. Then he said: "Well, I see no reason why you shouldn't have access to the manuscript. Excuse my caution, but there are certain people who would like to get their hands on it for the wrong reasons. I'll write you a note authorising you to look at it."

After writing me the note he saw me to the door and shook hands once again before I left. I walked down the street into a main thoroughfare where I boarded a tram to return to the city.

Next morning I returned to the library, presented the note and sat down to wait for the manuscript to be brought to me. After half an hour Dr. Krassny appeared with a concerned frown on her face. "I'm terribly sorry, Mr. Cairns," she said "but the manuscript seems to have disappeared. It's not on the shelves where it should be. We'll continue looking in case it has been misplaced. In the meantime is there anything else you would like to look at?"

I said I would like to see anything on alchemy or the Rosicrucians, and for the next few hours I worked my way through a pile of manuscripts of the same genre as the *Treasure House* but found nothing about the sword or the elixir. Half way through the afternoon I left for my tea appointment with Fräulein Weiss.

I reached the Café Zimmermann with a quarter of an hour to spare. It was a café of the cosy old Viennese type with red velvet upholstery and newspapers on sticks for the customers to read. I picked up a daily paper, settled myself at a table near the door and waited. Five minutes before the appointed time a young woman entered and walked straight up to my table.

"Mr. Cairns," she said, without any question in her voice, "I'm very glad to meet you." Something about her made me trust her immediately. She was small, dark and in about her mid-thirties, and was dressed in a blue coat and white fur hat. In the Kärntnerstrasse she might have passed as any other rich young Viennese woman, but seen close to she had some quality that singled her out. It may have been the combination of the slight severity of her face with its close-cropped fringe of hair and the intent look in her dark eyes.

"How did you know me so easily?" I asked after we had ordered tea and cakes.

"I will tell you that later," she said. "We have much to talk about, but this café is not a suitable place. When we have had tea we shall go back to my flat. But I didn't want to ask you there without seeing you first."

So over tea she told me about herself. She was Jewish on her mother's side, and when Hitler had taken over Austria the family had emigrated to Britain and ended up in a suburb of Edinburgh where she had spent her formative years. When she spoke English it was with a genteel Scottish accent. She hinted that it was from her father, a doctor, that she had inherited her occult interests. Soon after the war both her parents died, and, having no family ties she set off for India where she spent two years learning yoga. Then she came back to Vienna and set up as a yoga teacher.

When we had finished tea and paid the bill between us she drove me in her car to her flat in the Schüttelstrasse which had a view over the Danube Canal. All the furniture in it had the legs cut off a few inches from the ground, and she explained that this was because it was healthier to sit near the floor. The living quarters consisted of a small bedroom, kitchen and corridor, all crammed with books, paintings, and objects such as pebbles and rusty iron keys arranged in artistic little groups. The entire front of the apartment was given over to a large bare room in which she gave her lessons. In the corner of this we sat down on low chairs by a table with a simple Japanese arrangement of twigs in a vase and a stick of incense which she had set burning.

"Now," she began, "I can tell you how I recognized you. It's very simple. You are one of us. I can tell that you have not been so for long. You have not yet developed the sensitivity to recognize another initiate, but it will come. Now I want to hear of your interest in the manuscript."

I told her the story of how I had lost North's copy of the document on the underground and how I had discovered that other thefts of similar manuscripts had been reported. Then I told her of North's theory that L.O.Q. was behind it and that he was seeking something of importance in the stolen manuscripts. I explained that I had come to Vienna to examine the only known copy of the *Treasure House* to try and find out where the sword was located and what else L.O.Q. might be looking for in the manuscript. I told her about Professor Irtenkauf and how the manuscript had suddenly gone missing.

At that point she looked extremely worried. She stood up and paced up and down the room.

"Do you think the manuscript's been stolen?" I asked.

"I don't think it, I know it."

She walked over to the window and drew the curtains across the dusk and the lights on the other side of the canal. Then she came back and sat in the pool of the light cast by the table lamp. Except for the faint rumble of traffic in the street we could have been thousands of miles from Vienna, in some Buddhist temple in the Himalayas.

"Did you read enough of the manuscript," she asked "to come across a reference to the Elixir of Concentrated Energy?"

I nodded.

"Well that is what your friend L.O.Q. is looking for – that and the Sword of Power. We believe he is in league with one of the intelligence services of the Soviet bloc, probably the KGB – we have our sources in those countries. Probably the deal is that he gets the Sword and they get the Elixir. Once they have the Elixir and know how to mix it with certain other substances they will be have what we call the Stone of Infinite Force – something like nuclear power only greater. Do you follow?"

"Only too well. Is there any danger of their finding these things?"

"Not as long as they remain in the safekeeping of the Brotherhood."

"By the Brotherhood you mean the Rosicrucians?"

She shrugged her shoulders. "The Rosicrucian Order is only one branch of the thing to which you and I both belong: the Brotherhood of Light. Here we call ourselves Rosicrucians because that happens to be our tradition."

"And you have this substance that can generate infinite force?"

"Not the substance but the ingredient without which it cannot be made, the Elixir. The other ingredients are such as can be bought over the counter in any chemist's shop, and the preparation is child's play when you know the technique – it can be done in any kitchen. But

129

without the Elixir the substance has no power. A small quantity of this Elixir exists in our chief vault here in Vienna. Other people knew of its existence – Hitler for instance. He ordered Himmler to use his Gestapo to get hold of every alchemical book he could find and to arrest and interrogate alchemists and occultists of every description to see if any clue could be found. He also used his own occultists to try and track down the Elixir by magical means, but he failed. Had he come anywhere near finding it, we were ready to destroy the last stocks of it in existence. As for the Sword, an attempt was once made to penetrate our vault to steal it, but the culprit was killed by the barriers guarding the vault." I guessed she was referring to François de Carnac, but said nothing.

"Now," she went on, "it is clear from what you have told me that another attempt on the vault is being planned, perhaps a more powerful attempt than before. I must warn the lodge straight away."

She went into one of the back rooms and put through a call to someone who seemed to be a bookseller. I heard her ask if he had any incunabula for sale. Then she came back and said that she was to leave for the lodge straight away and that I must come with her.

Travelling on foot, we crossed the canal and made our way through quiet side streets until we were standing in an alleyway before a decrepit shop front that advertised itself in faded letters above the door as the premises of Wolfgang Kurz, antiquarian bookseller. Although it was nearing seven o'clock and the shop was officially closed, we pushed open the door to find ourselves in a room only about ten feet across but enormously high and long, with books on shelves up to the ceiling and on a narrow table down the middle.

A little grey-haired man was sitting at a desk near the door, reading by the light of a green-shaded lamp. He rose as we came in and took off his gold-rimmed spectacles. He was slightly stooped and had about him the air of comfortable and scholarly shabbiness that seems to characterize men of his trade.

"Good evening, Herr Kurz," said Helga.

The bookseller seemed to be expecting us and nodded affably. "You rang about the incunabula. Let's go down to the basement and see what we can find."

He locked the door and led us to the back of the shop where a rickety stair led down into another roomful of books. But we did not linger there to look at incunabula. The old man swung back a section of bookshelf revealing a doorway leading to another flight of stairs that descended sideways. He switched on an electric light, and we followed him down into a short, stone-flagged corridor at the end of which was another door. He opened this and ushered us into a room that reminded me of North's temple under his house at Ravenhurst. There were the same rich hangings, the same faint whiff of incense. The cloth behind the altar, however, was embroidered not with a pentagram but with a red rose on a cross of gold. But the main thing that distinguished this vault from the other temple was that down the wall on the left-hand side there ran a bench covered with retorts, test-tubes, flasks, Bunsen burners, crucibles and rows of jars containing chemicals of different colours.

When I had taken all this in I turned to look at the bookseller and it was then that I noticed with a shock of surprise the change that had come over him. He seemed to have grown in height and become younger. His stoop had gone and he carried himself with an air of authority. When he spoke it was not with the voice of a comfortable old bookseller but with the firm tone of one accustomed to command.

"Welcome brother," he said to me, after Helga had introduced us. Then he turned to her and asked what news she brought.

Speaking with deference she told him about North and his manuscript and how others of the same type had been stolen and how the copy in the National Library had gone missing. She said she was sure that L.O.Q. and his friends from the communist bloc were behind the thefts and they were looking for the sword and the elixir.

He listened gravely and then nodded. "You were right to come. It may be that this time we shall have to destroy the elixir." He walked over to the laboratory bench and picked up a small phial containing a greenish liquid. It glinted and changed colour subtly as he held it closer for me to see. "No doubt you are wondering," he said "why we keep this powerful elixir without using it to prepare the Stone of Infinite Force. There are two reasons. Firstly, the Stone of Infinite Force is also infinitely dangerous. Secondly, the Elixir has another use. It is because of this Elixir that I am alive today. I am not permitted to tell you my exact age, but I can tell you that it was I who prevented the Elixir from falling into the hands of Napoleon. Only the Imperator of our order is permitted to use it to prolong life, but small amounts have been used to cure illness in cases where the Brotherhood has deemed it necessary."

He replaced the phial on the bench, then turned back to me. "You see that I am speaking freely to you," he went on. "That is because your coming is not entirely unexpected. Our sacred books tell of a time when the mission with which we are entrusted shall pass from us to another centre of initiation. We have many treasures, but two above all. One is the Elixir. The other, as you know, is the Sword of Power. To understand that power you must know the sword's history. You have heard of King Arthur's Excalibur."

"Yes," I said, "the sword that came out of a lake and returned there after King Arthur died."

He nodded. "That is the legend, and behind it there lies a truth. There was a sword which was owned by the figure whom we know as Arthur. You see Arthur was in fact a Romanized Britain who was an initiate of an old mystery cult which masqueraded behind Christian symbolism, or rather adapted the symbolism to its own meaning. The sword was the symbol of his spiritual power, and as long as he remained pure in spirit it remained with him and served him. The cult of which he was an initiate practised a form of exalted sex magic in which Queen Guinevere was the supreme adept and High Priestess. But Arthur forgot the purpose of the magic and began to want Guinevere for her own sake. He became jealous of another man, Sir Lancelot, whom Guinevere had also initiated, and he denounced Lancelot as an adulterer. From that moment on his power declined, and he was eventually fatally wounded in battle.

"After Arthur's death the sword remained a symbol of the mystery cult. But in Britain the cult died out, and the sword passed to the continent of Europe where groups of initiates were still active. The Knights Templar were such a group. They possessed the sword for a time and guarded it in their stronghold in Palestine. Evil forces within the Church conspired to bring about the downfall of the Templars, and at the beginning of the 14th century the order was dissolved, its lands confiscated and its Grand Master, Jacques de Molay, burned at the stake. But the order did not die. A group of initiates fled to Arabia taking the sword with them and established a new centre there working closely with the Islamic sages. It was to this centre that the founder of our brotherhood, Christian Rosenkreuz, came on his journey to the Middle East. He remained there for a time and became a full initiate of the Templars who gave him authority to return to Germany and set up a branch of the order there. Later the Arabian centre was forced to close through persecution, and the sword itself was brought to Germany.

"Christian Rosenkreuz set up his brotherhood on the same principles as the Arthurian cult and the Templars – that is he practised the universal mystery religion, but presented it in Christian terms. He died in 1484, but by that time he had already sown the seeds of a great spiritual awakening that manifested itself externally as the Reformation. After his death the brotherhood continued its work and still continues it today.

"But we have always known that we possess only a part of the secret knowledge which will one day usher in a new golden age for mankind. That is why we were powerless to prevent the holocaust of the Third Reich and the Second World War. Hitler and his colleagues had the full force of the Satanic powers behind them, while we had only a part of the powers of good behind us.

"You see the sword represents one of the four cornerstones of magical power, symbolized in the suits of the Tarot and the four sacred objects of the Grail legends. The other three are the wand or lance, the dish, or pentacle, and the cup or grail. Had Arthur retained his spiritual leadership for long enough he would have brought all four together, and Britain would have become a great centre of spiritual power that would have shed its light throughout the world. As it was, he failed, and the world remained in darkness. But according to our traditions Britain is still the womb out of which the New Age will grow. And it is to Britain that all four objects must one day return. In case that day should come soon, it is as well that you should know of the existence of this sword."

With that he walked over to the wall against which the altar stood and lifted aside the cloth with the rose cross on it. Behind was a door in the stonework which swung open as he touched it. He reached inside, and a moment later was holding in his right had a sword in a golden sheath. He drew it out, and I saw that the steel blade was chased with strange characters similar to those I had seen on North's pentacle. The pommel was of gold, and the hilt of some gleaming blue enameled material. He put it back in its sheath and handed it to me. It was small, but heavy, and as I took it I felt again the sensation that I was holding something with great power and something almost with a will of its own.

He saw my reaction and said: "You understand why this sword

must be kept in the hands of the initiated. If need be it may be your task to take it back on its final journey to Britain."

He took the sword back, and just as he had finished replacing it in its safe in the wall there came the sound of a gently tinkling bell from somewhere overhead. The old man listened. "There's someone at the shop door," he said. "Strange. I wonder who it could be at this hour. I had better go and see." He beckoned us to follow him out of the vault.

When we reached the upper basement he told us to wait and went on up into the shop. We heard him unlocking the front door and telling whoever the caller was that the shop was closed. Then the unknown person spoke in a voice that immediately made me listen intently. It addressed the shopkeeper in good German but with a slight English accent and in a tone that was familiar to me from somewhere.

"I know that voice," I whispered to Helga, "but I can't pin it down."

"Try," she said. "It may be important."

I listened again and heard the caller saying: "I'll come back tomorrow then. Sorry to have troubled you."

It was only when he had gone that I realized the feeling of evil that had been present while he was there. It was a relief to hear the bookseller locking the front door again and coming back down the stairs.

Helga immediately told him that I had found the man's voice vaguely familiar, and Herr Kurz asked me to try my utmost to remember where I had heard it. I tried, but it was no use. The voice had rung only the merest hint of a bell in my mind.

"What did he look like?" I asked.

"A large, powerfully built man, with a heavy beard and moustache, in about his mid 40s. But with his kind appearances don't count. If we saw him again he could look totally different."

"Then you think," said Helga, "that he was someone of high degree in the Black Brotherhood?"

"Not merely someone of high degree," Herr Kurz replied. "It is probable that that was L.O.Q. himself. He may have found out that the vault is here. If so he will probably come back with his KGB friends. We must take no chances. The treasures must be removed and the vault must be closed."

We were still standing in the lower basement, and Herr Kurz once more opened the door leading down to the vault. As he did so there came a tremendous crash from upstairs. A second later I realized that it must have been caused by the shop door being broken in, for all at once the floor above resounded with the noise of many footsteps.

"Quick," said Herr Kurz, "into the vault!"

He held the door open while we entered the stairway. Up above we heard a voice shout, "Over here!" And the outline of a figure appeared at the top of the stairs leading into the shop. Herr Kurz shut the door and followed us down the stairs, but he had given our position away. We had just reached the bottom of the stairs when our pursuers managed to open the door and came down after us.

I have only confused memories of what happened after that. We found ourselves in the vault, and behind us a voice shouted: "Stay where you are, all of you! We are armed!" Then the vault seemed to be full of men with close-cropped hair and cold, hard faces. Two of them appeared to be in command. One of them was small and thin and wore dark glasses and a leather coat. The other was fat and had on a light-coloured raincoat and a hat with a narrow brim. "Stay where you are," the fat one repeated, then barked to his men: "Search the premises!"

Meanwhile the small, thin KGB agent – for that's what I took him and the others to be – had walked over to the laboratory bench. But before he could do anything more the old bookseller had rushed over to the bench and picked up the phial with the green liquid in it. The agent made a grab for the phial, but the old man was too quick for him. He dashed the thing violently against the stone floor, and from the place where it fell there welled up suddenly a cloud of green vapor accompanied by a powerful smell, pungent, slightly sweet, and choking. The cloud grew until it filled the whole room, and from the place where the broken phial lay what seemed to be a concentrated ball of green force had formed, sending out billows of vapour that made me gasp for breath. I could see that it had rendered the KGB agents helpless. Some were coughing violently, others cowering against the walls covering their faces with their hands.

Then I became aware that there were other figures in the room, not struck helpless by the green mist but moving through it as though in their element. They were animate, yet strangely fluid, like pieces of living jelly seeking a form. As they came near the pulsating green centre they achieved for a moment a sharper definition which they lost as they drew back from it again.

The room was now filled with the shouts and screams of the terrified KGB men. Some of them were groping toward the door seeking escape. In the confusion, I saw the old bookseller stagger toward the altar, draw back the cloth and open the safe containing the sword. He took out the weapon and then turned toward me. As he did so, I saw with a shock that he had changed almost beyond recognition. His hair had gone pure white and his face was lined and emaciated—the face of a man infinitely old. He came toward the place were Helga and I were standing and, with great effort, pulled us toward the back of the vault. He pressed against the stonework, and a door opened. Before he thrust us through the doorway, I saw that the green ball of vapour had turned into a kind of fountain which spurted outward with ever-increasing force and with a kind of angry hiss.

Then we were through the doorway and into a sort of small vestibule with another door facing us. This second door was opened by the old man, and we found ourselves breathing fresh air. For a few minutes the relief was so great that I did not notice our surroundings. Then I saw that we were in what appeared to be an underground car park, the kind that might serve a large office building or apartment block.

The old man thrust the sword into my hands. "The time has come," he said in a faint, hoarse voice. "Take the sword to England. I must return to complete the destruction of the vault." Then he disappeared again through the doorway by which we had come.

Helga seemed to know the lie of the land. We took possession of a large black Mercedes that was parked nearby, and in another minute we had emerged from a ramp into the streets. We drove until we found a public telephone box, and Helga made me wait in the car while she made some calls. Then she got back into the car and we drove to Vienna airport in time to catch a midnight charter flight to London. At the airport she said goodbye, having assured me that my journey back would go smoothly. And it did. No questions were asked about my strange burden, and the airline staff seemed more than usually solicitous. One of them provided a large cardboard box for me to carry the sword in. I was allowed to take it into the cabin and place it in the luggage compartment.

During the flight I grew increasingly nervous about getting the sword through British Customs. I decided it would be safer to declare it, so at Heathrow I left the baggage hall through the exit marked "Goods to declare" and showed the sword to a tall, middle-aged customs officer with a brisk, military manner and a moustache to go with it.

Holding up the sword, he said: "Weapons are supposed to be accompanied by a special import certificate."

"But this isn't a weapon," I blurted out, unable to think of anything else to say.

"Oh? What is it then?" he said with a touch of sarcasm.

"It's for ceremonial purposes."

"You mean in a lodge?"

"You could say that, yes."

"Ah!" His eyes lit up. "So it's a masonic sword is it? In that case I won't insist on a certificate." He winked and tapped the tide of his nose with his finger. "You can go on through."

Within a few hours of arriving back in London I was at Ravenhurst recounting the whole affair to North. For once I sensed that he seemed surprised by the way things had turned out. When I had finished he said: "It seems that you and I have been given an important task. We must place the sword along with the pentacle behind magical barriers." Together we went down to his temple, and I watched him perform a complicated ritual which ended with the sword being placed in a stone recess below the altar. King Arthur's Excalibur had come home at last.

Three months later, in the springtime, I went back to Vienna to write an article for my magazine. The chestnuts were in bloom in the Prater, and horse-drawn carriages were conveying tourists along the Ringstrasse. Frau Schneider was still running her pension, and gave me my old room to stay in. On my arrival I telephoned Helga's flat, but a strange voice informed me that she had gone away and left no forwarding address. Later I managed to find the alleyway where the bookshop had been, but the building had completely vanished, and I saw that some kind of building work was going on behind a temporary wooden fence. I looked through a gap in the fence. Where the basement and the vault had been there was nothing but a large pit dropping down about forty feet and ending in mud. One of the men working on the site told me that it was a shaft for the new underground railway. "And what was here before?" I asked him.

He shrugged. "Some derelict old shop. Apparently it was ripe for demolition anyway. Bit of luck, really."

9

That summer a funfair came to Gorehamstead and took over a park. There were dodgem cars, rifle-shooting booths, a carrousel, a haunted house and stalls selling ice cream, rock and candy floss. I went there with Mark and Sally one Saturday afternoon. As a child I had gone to similar fairs, enticed by the brassy music, the brightly painted stalls, the bustle, the brash energy. But always I had come away disappointed. After you had buffeted your way around the dodgems, made yourself dizzy on the carrousel and won some piece of imitation jewellery at the shooting range, you felt you had spent your money for nothing.

Mark, however, was entranced by it all. I watched him throw coconuts, ride a carrousel horse and giggle with delight in a room lined with distorting mirrors. There was also a Punch and Judy show and, standing apart at the edge of the park, a Gypsy caravan where you could have your fortune told.

"I'll go with Mark to the Punch and Judy show," Sally said. "Why don't you try the Gypsy fortune-teller?"

I laughed. "That charlatan!" But out of curiosity I strolled towards the caravan. It was the old-fashioned kind with brightly painted woodwork and steps leading up to an open doorway. A sign above the doorway said: "Gypsy Casimira, palmist, Tarot reader, clairvoyant. Your future told for fifty pence." Gypsy Casimira herself was sitting on the steps – a stage Gypsy with long, curly black hair, wearing enormous brass earrings, a red silk head scarf and a long, loose, shawl with a bright floral pattern.

As I approached the caravan I heard a burst of accordion music behind me and turned to see a group of six Morris dancers taking up their positions for a performance – big, lusty men in white shirts and trousers, with red criss-crossing sashes across their chests and bell-pads strapped to their legs below the knee. On their heads they wore straw hats with flowers around the brim. Each carried a sturdy wooden stick. The accordionist was a stocky, bearded man in a red waistcoat, baggy yellow trousers and a black top hat. Completing the group was the Fool, a figure wearing a jester's cap and a long tunic covered with snippets of cloth of many colours, and carrying a smaller stick with a blown-up balloon tied to the end. The musician paused, then began to play a springing, hopping tune and the dancers sprang and hopped with it, forming circles, weaving around each other, changing places, clashing their sticks together or banging them against the ground. The Fool danced around them, exaggeratedly imitating their movements and occasionally striking them with the balloon.

"They're dancing the eternal dance," the Gypsy woman said. "It's the dance that folk have been dancing since Adam and Eve to keep the world turning. Their feet move to the rhythm of nature and their staves are offspring of the one staff, the rod that Moses carried when he led the children of Israel out of Egypt. See how they strike them against the ground. Thus did Moses strike the waters of the Nile to turn them into blood. Thus did he strike the rock of Horeb and cause fresh water to flow forth. And before Moses the rod was carried by the god Thoth and after him by the Wandering Jew Ahasver, and then it passed through many hands until came to be possessed by us, the Romanies. Come, I will show it to you, but first I shall read your cards."

I held up my hand to refuse, but she said: "There'll be no charge. I've been expecting you."

I wanted to turn and walk away, but instead I found myself going closer to the caravan. The woman smiled as though aware that she had some secret power over me. She stepped inside and I followed her into a curtained-off compartment, hung with dark blue cloth embroidered with stars, planets and a moon in silver thread. On a table covered with a purple velvet cloth were a crystal ball, a pack of Tarot cards and a lighted candle in a brass candlestick. She waved me to a chair and took another one on the opposite side of the table, then she fanned out the cards and invited me to pick one.

From outside came the sounds of the Morris men – the merry tune, the clashing of the sticks and the jingling of the bells. I was anxious to get back to Sally and Mark, but I decided to humour her.

"Ah, the Fool!" she said as I laid it face up on the table. "Of course! That is you."

I looked at the card and saw a young man in a gaily patterned tunic, walking through a mountainous landscape under a brilliant sun, with a small, prancing dog at his heels. Over one shoulder he carried a stick from which hung a crude bag, presumably for his few possessions. He was walking blithely towards the edge of a precipice, his gaze fixed on something high up and far away. I no longer heard the Morris men or the noise of the funfair. My eyes were riveted to the card. The precipice and the mountainous landscape immediately reminded me of the nightmare that had brought me to Gilbert. I began to feel dizzy and, as though from far away, I heard the Gypsy woman go on speaking.

"You're a young man striding along on a quest for your life's meaning – or rather dancing, like the Fool in the Morris dance, who is not a fool at all. You are approaching a chasm, which I think you recognize, because you have already faced it once, if I am right?" She looked up at me with her dark, mascara-ringed eyes, then back at the card. "But you are not walking blindly over the edge. Rather your higher self has already taken flight over the chasm. It's a kind of initiation ... an initiation into a certain order." Her hand, heavy with jewelled rings, moved over the card. "You see the rose that he carries in his left hand. That is the sign of the order, called by some the Rosicrucians. You have made good progress in the order, but you still have some way to go. Now draw another card."

I obeyed. When I turned up the card I saw that it showed a man in a white robe, facing a kind of altar. In his hand he held a short wand, and on the table lay a larger wand, a sword, a chalice and a disc with a pentagram inscribed on it.

"The Magician!" Casimira said. "He is your mentor. He is already an adept of the order, and he will show you the way forward. You see the roses and lilies in the foreground – again symbols of the Rosicrucian order. Now look at the objects on the altar – the disc or talisman, the sword, the chalice and the rod or wand – the four great magical weapons corresponding to the four elements. Your mentor has two of them and is seeking the others. Now draw again."

This time I drew the Ace of Wands, showing a hand emerging from a cloud and holding a piece of branch still putting out leaves. In the distant background was a castle on a hilltop.

Casimira's eyes lit up. "The cards are speaking loud and clear. The second card shows the four magical weapons. This one shows the wand alone. It signifies the start of a great enterprise ... an enterprise connected with a great house – that's the castle on the hill. It's like the Grail Castle, Monsalvat, from which the Knights of the Grail ride out into the world to do great deeds. Your mentor is a modern Grail King. He already has the talisman and sword. The chalice will soon come his way. The time has come for him to possess the wand ... wait here."

She drew aside the star-spangled curtain, disappeared into the front part of the caravan and came back holding a long wooden box like the kind that a musician might use for carrying a flute or an oboe. She opened the lid and drew out the wand. It was about two feet long and made of wood with a reddish tinge, engraved near the tip with the Hebrew letter *shin* and, lower down, a fire-breathing dragon whose tail curled around the shaft. The tip was a ruby held in place by a brass ring. When she handed it to me I felt awed. The ruby glowed and sparkled in the candlelight. The wood felt warm and alive.

"It is a gift," the Gypsy said "and yet, like all the best gifts, it deserves a gift in return."

Gilbert would surely want me to acquire the wand, I thought, but I had no way of knowing how much it was worth.

"Would ten pounds be all right as the return gift?" I asked.

She pursed her lips and eyed me for a moment. "Perhaps not quite ..."

"Fifteen?"

She nodded, replaced the wand in the box and handed it to me.

"Tell you mentor to use it wisely," she called after me as I left the caravan.

I circumvented the Morris men and pushed my way through the crowd towards the Punch and Judy booth, where the show had just ended. When Mark had finished telling me excitedly about the puppet show, he asked me what was in the box. "A magic wand," I said and opened the lid.

"Good heavens," Sally said. "Did you get that from the Gypsy woman? How much did you pay for it?"

"Fifteen pounds."

"What? Fifteen pounds for that piece of junk!" She sounded shocked.

Seeing the wand in the daylight, I began to feel that I had been cheated. The ruby was obviously just a piece of coloured glass, and the engraving on the shaft had been crudely burnt in, probably with a soldering iron. But Mark was impressed by the wand. "What can it do?" he asked.

"We'll see when we get it home," I told him.

I had intended to give the wand to North, but now I was sure he would laugh at me when he saw it. The wand was just a cheap conjurer's prop, and the Gypsy woman had made a fool of me. Her Tarot reading had been remarkably accurate, but I told myself that it had simply been a mixture of chance and clever guesswork.

When we got home I stuck the wand into the umbrella stand by the front door, telling Mark that he could play with it after tea. But later, when he went to fetch it, he came back saying that the wand had disappeared. I went to the umbrella stand and, sure enough, there was no sign of it.

"Well, it's a magic wand," I said jokingly but with an uneasy feeling. "It's probably hiding somewhere."

I found it several days later in the attic, when I went up there with a torch to look for some old family papers. There it was lying on a trunk, the red stone catching the light from my torch.

"You'd better give it to Gilbert," Sally said "as the Gypsy wanted you to do."

So that same evening, a Sunday, I drove to Ravenhurst with the wand and told North the whole story.

"Remarkable!" North said, holding the tip of the wand up the light. "You were wrong to suppose that the stone is a fake. You see those fine lines of deeper red. They're traces of a different mineral called rutile, which is found in all natural rubies."

"But a ruby that size must be worth a fortune!" I gasped.

"Yes. You got a bargain. And the decoration on the shaft, that you thought was done with a soldering iron, is in fact very old – possibly many centuries. You can tell by how worn it is in places. You did the right thing to buy it from the Gypsy and bring it to me. Now we have the third member of the Tetrad. The Fourth will come our way sooner or later."

10

The more I became involved with North and his world the more difficult it became for me to adjust to the periods of everyday routine. This was made all the harder by the fact that, apart from Sally, there was no one I could talk to about the occult side of my life – least of all Simon Freeman with whom I shared an office at work. He was the antithesis of myself: a down-to-earth, exuberant extrovert, quick-witted and intelligent, but uninterested in the world of theory. Although our temperaments were so different, we got on well together, and he was a valuable counterbalance to the other side of my life. He had a teasing manner which was very effective in removing people's inhibitions, and which he found useful with women. He could also be moody and vacillating, and he was continually complaining that his job as letters editor on the *Townsman* did not satisfy his ambitions.

When he was away from the office I found myself missing his grumbling, his mimicry and his frequent outbursts of good-natured aggression. On my own I often found that a strange form of lethargy would come over me, a sensation of being a detached observer temporarily resident in this body, this tweed jacket, these hands and shirt-cuffs on the desk before me, listening through these borrowed ears to the shouts of the porters in the vegetable market outside, looking through these alien eyes out of the window across the rooftops to the Royal Opera House. At such times I found that to perform a task such as looking up a name in the telephone directory involved a major effort of will.

I found myself in such a mood one Friday morning when Simon was late because of an appointment with the dentist. I was having a cup of coffee to postpone beginning work when the telephone rang and I heard North's familiar voice on the other end of the line.

"Can you come round to Ravenhurst tomorrow afternoon?" he asked. "I have a small group of people coming for a little experiment and would like you to take part."

I asked him what it was all about, but he would not give me any details. There was a long background story which he evidently could not tell me over the telephone.

"All right," I said, and we arranged that I should arrive at tea time the following day.

By the time I put down the telephone I was intrigued as to what North had up his sleeve, and the prospect enabled me to face the morning's work rather more energetically. At eleven o'clock Simon came in. His first action after bidding me good morning was to stride over to the wastepaper basket and toss a handful of halfpennies into it.

"Blasted nuisance, these new halfpennies," he said. "They fill your pockets and you can't do anything with them." I could see that the dentist had not left him in a good mood. Then minutes later Maureen, a tall, skinny, harsh-voiced office-girl came in and demanded her weekly "tea money". Simon cursed that he had forgotten it was Friday and was forced to fish his coppers out again. "Tea money" was a system whereby Maureen and another girl, Susan, collected twenty-five pence a week from every member of the staff in return for providing coffee in the morning and tea in the afternoon. This catering service seemed to occupy their entire time, but at least it was better than having a vending machine.

Simon sat down and began to sift through the day's batch of letters, separating them into two folders marked "accept" and "reject". Most of them were decided on at a glance, but one letter he read twice through and then tossed it over to me.

"You're the occult expert around here, aren't you?" he said. "See what you make of that. Is it sane enough to publish, or is the man completely round the bend? I'll leave it with you to read."

I picked up the letter. It was from a Dr. Obadiah Tillit, of Dorchester, Dorset, and was written in black ink in a small, clear, and careful hand. It read as follows:

"Dear Sir,

I am writing to you with an enquiry which is perhaps a somewhat unusual one for the pages of a journal such as yours, but I very much hope that your readers will be able to help. My enquiry concerns a lost object, and it is necessary that I relate how the object was acquired.

"Before the war my wife and I were on holiday in Rome and toward the end of our stay were looking around the shops for some memento of our holiday to take home. We were passing a junk shop in an old

151

side street when something in the window caught my eye. It was a kind of shallow bowl or cup make of some dull metal, possibly pewter, with a short, trumpet-shaped stem. The shape was most attractive, and the outside of the rim was chased with an unusual flowing pattern which rather reminded me of the serpent motifs that you find on Celtic monuments. We went into the shop and asked to see it. When the shopkeeper handed it to us I saw that the inside of the bowl was enameled in such a way that the colour was deep blue at the centre, becoming paler toward the edges.

"Neither of us had seen anything quite like it before, and I asked the shopkeeper what it was and where it had come from. He told us that it had come into his possession in mysterious circumstances. The day before it had been brought into the shop by a man dressed in a grey robe with a hood, whom the shopkeeper had assumed to be some kind of monk. The man had handed him the vessel and told him that he wanted it to be sold, but required no payment for it. Then he had disappeared. As to the history or origin of the thing the shopkeeper knew nothing. He quoted us a reasonable price, so we bought the object and brought it home.

"Now comes the part of the story that you may find difficult to believe, but I assure you that I am a down-to-earth medical man not given to flights of fancy, and I still cannot explain the events that occurred. When we returned we placed the cup on the mantlepiece in our living room here in Dorchester. Immediately it began to do strange things. For one thing it kept moving its position in the room. At first it only did this overnight, but later it would do it during the day when we were out of the room for a few minutes. Then one day we actually saw it move. It rose from the mantlepiece and floated across the room to the bookcase. If it was what is sometimes called a poltergeist that was responsible, then the creature was somehow associated with the cup, for no other object was involved.

"Besides the moving about, the cup also sometimes made a low humming noise at night. And when I woke up to this noise I invariably found that I had been having strange dreams. In one of these dreams I saw standing by my bed the figure of a man dressed in a grey robe – it was only later that I came to identify him with the monk described by the Rome shopkeeper, for my first impression of him was not of a monk, but more of a high priest, someone commanding and authoritative.

"In his left hand he was holding the cup. With his right he beckoned to me to follow him. I did so and we moved toward the door which had transformed itself into a great stone pylon, the other side of which was veiled by a misty darkness. We passed through the gateway and emerged suddenly into daylight. Looking around, I saw that we were in an area of green fields, hedgerows and winding roads. My companion handed me the cup and beckoned again. I followed him over the countryside until we were standing at the intersection of two footpaths beside which stood an upright stone, some six feet high, crudely hewn into a point as though by some prehistoric people. Close beside the stone grew an old thorn tree which rose two or three feet higher and whose branches hid the lower part of the stone. My companion pulled aside the branches, and I saw that in the part of the stone which was revealed, close to the ground, a deep recess had been cut. He indicated by his gestures that he wished the cup to be placed in the recess, and I obeyed. My arm disappeared up to the elbow as I thrust the vessel into the stone. When it was in place my companion let the thorn branches spring back into place, and the hiding place was concealed again. It was only then that, looking up, I saw rising up near by the unmistakable outline of Glastonbury Tor. Then the dream faded, and I found myself awake in my bedroom with that humming noise still coming up from the living room below.

"The message of the dream was clear to part of my mind. The vessel was in some way restless and needed to be returned to its rightful place which evidently was in the stone that I had been shown by the man in the grey robe. I say a part of my mind recognized this; but the dominant part – the practical medical man – rejected it as being unscientific nonsense. I had to experience the same dream several times more before I decided, for the sake of peace of mind, to try and find the stone and return the cup to it. I drove to Glastonbury with the vessel and, with the aid of an Ordnance Survey map, looked for places near the Tor where footpaths intersected. It did not take me long to find the place, which was exactly as I had seen it in the dream. That in itself shook my scepticism, and without any further delay I found the recess and placed the vessel in it, having first wrapped it in linen for protection. I returned home and experienced no more disturbing dreams or phenomena. It was a great relief to both my wife and myself, and I was sure that I had done the right thing.

"I forgot all about the incident until last month when I was in

London for a few days to attend a medical conference. One late afternoon I was walking down Chancery Lane and saw in the window of a jeweller's shop what appeared to be the selfsame vessel, or at least a very accurate copy. It was after closing time, otherwise I would have gone into the shop to ask about the object. For some reason it made me uneasy to think that the cup might have been moved from Glastonbury. As it was, I had to return to the shop the following morning. But when I arrived the vessel had disappeared from the window, and the shopkeeper told me that it had been bought only a matter of minutes earlier by a man whom he described as being about sixty, short, and powerfully built, with sharp features and a full head of grey hair, dressed in a suit of brown Harris tweed. I thanked the shopkeeper and set off down Chancery Lane in the direction I was told the man had gone, but I reached the corner of Chancery Lane without seeing any sign of him.

"As soon as I returned to the West Country I went back to Glastonbury and looked in the stone. There was no sign of the vessel. I concluded that somehow it had found its way to the shop in Chancery Lane. The shopkeeper, by the way, said that he had bought it from a dealer at Bermondsey market who had no idea where it came from. Someone must have found it by accident and sold it.

"You may wonder why I am still concerned about the vessel's whereabouts. I can only say that I have an instinctive feeling that the object has some supernatural power and would like to know if its present owner has experienced similar phenomena to those witnessed by me. I should also like to know if the reader can throw some light on the whole strange story.

Yours sincerely,

Obadiah Tillit."

When I had finished reading the letter, Simon asked me what I made of it. I told him that I found it fascinating and that the man did not strike me as being a lunatic. But I asked if I could show it to a friend of mine who knew more about this sort of thing than I did. He agreed.

The next day I took the letter with me when I went to visit North. Diana opened the door and said: "Come through to the drawing room, Paul. Hugh Rhys-Morgan, our vicar, is here already talking to Gilbert. We're just about to have tea."

In the drawing room North was sitting talking to a middle-aged man dressed in a dark suit and dog collar. They both stood up as I came in, and North introduced me to the vicar.

"Glad to meet you," said Rhys-Morgan in a strong Welsh accent, grasping my hand firmly.

We all sat down, North on the sofa and Rhys-Morgan and I in the two arm chairs by the fireplace, while Mrs. North handed us tea and cakes.

"It's Hugh we have to thank for this little gathering," North explained to me; then, turning to the vicar, he said: "Paul might as well hear the story before your friend arrives."

Rhys-Morgan leant back and lit a cigarette, then inhaled deeply before he spoke. "It's a curious tale," he said, slipping easily into the role of raconteur. He had the sort of face and voice that hold the attention without effort – the face rugged and furrowed with dark, bushy eyebrows and deep-set brown eyes; the voice deep, lilting and finely modulated. "Twenty years ago," he said, "I was a young curate in a village near Stroud in Gloucestershire, and one of my parishioners was a Scottish writer – perhaps you've heard of him – called Fergus Murray."

"Yes," I said. "A historical novelist, isn't he?"

"That's right, and a very successful one too. Even when I first knew him he was already a well-known name – he would have been about fifty then. When I try to describe what he was like 'recluse' is the first word that springs to mind. He lived in a small cottage outside the village and discouraged anyone coming to see him. He had a reputation for being irascible and quarrelsome – always having rows with his publishers, his agent, and anyone else who did business with him.

"The vicar warned me about him when I first came to the village, but strangely enough I got on well with Fergus from the start – I think I was about the only one in the village who did. We had something in common you see. We were both refugees from a puritan Celtic background, I from the valleys of Glamorgan and he from Argyll. And both of us had broken with our religious upbringing and become high churchmen. We shared a love of symbolism and ritual and a strong feeling for tradition.

"All this created quite a strong bond between us, and we enjoyed each other's company. I spent many an evening with him drinking his fine old Scotch whisky and talking by his fireside surrounded by piles of books. He was a very lively talker once he opened up, and he could go on for hours. The Celtic church was one of his favorite topics, and I think he probably knew every old stone cross in the country.

"Anyway, that was the side of him that I saw. Most other people only saw the quarrelsome, belligerent side. To tell you the truth, I think something embittered him earlier in life. He never told me what it was, but have a hunch it was something to do with a marriage that had broken up.

"After a couple of years I moved away to another part of the country. I continued to correspond with Fergus occasionally, but gradually we lost touch, the way one does. I did continue to read his books, though, and I gathered that they were selling increasingly well. I heard from other people that he had become even more eccentric. On the proceeds of his books he had bought a large Jacobean house not far from where he had lived before and built a private chapel on to it.

"I heard nothing more of him after that until about two weeks ago when quite out of the blue I received a letter from him telling me that he was coming to London for a few days and wanted to see me so that he could ask my advice about something. I telephoned him and we arranged to meet at his club in Pall Mall.

"I expected him to have changed in twenty years, but when I met him I saw that he hadn't changed in the way I expected. It wasn't exactly that he had mellowed with age – no it was more profound than that. The old bitter look had gone from his face completely, and he had a new kind of warmth and calm that seemed to indicate some deep inner change having taken place.

"I soon discovered the explanation. To cut a long story short, what had happened with him was this. One day, while he was praying in his private chapel he had a vision of an object – a sort of cup or vessel – which was standing in the window of a jeweller's shop in a London street which he recognized. The cup was bathed in light and seemed to him to be emitting some find form of energy. On the day following the dream he happened to be going to London, so he found the street and the shop. And sure enough, there in the window was the cup. Acting out of a strange compulsion he bought the thing, took it home and placed it in his private chapel. Every day he sat before it and prayed, and every time he did this he felt that some kind of beneficent force was flowing out of the object and into him. After a few weeks he began to feel that a permanent and deep-rooted change had taken place within him. He was convinced that the cup had some unique and spiritual power, and he wanted my opinion as to what the thing might be. To put it in plain language, he had begun to think that it might be the original Holy Grail, and he knew that I was one of the few churchmen who would not be scornful of such an idea. I had a look at it and come to the conclusion that I was out of my depth and that it was a matter for my friend Gilbert. Fergus is coming up from Gloucestershire today to stay at the vicarage with me. I told him to come straight on here when he arrived, so he should be here soon."

"Can you remember," I asked, "in which street the jeweller's shop was?"

"Yes," said Rhys-Morgan, "I believe it was Chancery Lane."

"I thought so," I said, and produced the letter from Dr. Tillit.

Rhys-Morgan read it in turn, and when North had finished he said: "Well, this is most remarkable. It appears that the gentleman in the tweed suit was in fact our Mr. Murray."

At that moment we heard the front doorbell ring, and Mrs. North went to answer it. "That should be Fergus now," said the vicar.

A few moments later Mrs. North ushered in a white-haired man of slightly less than average height, carrying a wooden box. He had a strong face, piercing blue eyes and a determined mouth. His expression was that of a man had been through years of struggle either with himself or with the world and had finally come to peace with both. His movements were quick and his manner alert. It was easy to see why his fellow men had found him intimidating. I knew him to be in his seventies, but he looked ten years younger.

Walking up to Rhys-Morgan he clasped the vicar's right hand in both of his and said in a strong Scottish accent: "Good to see you Hugh, good to see you." When he spoke I noticed for the first time the warmth which the vicar had told us about. He turned and shook hands with North and then with me while Rhys-Morgan introduced us. He placed the box on a small table beside the mantlepiece then sat down in a chair with a cup of tea which Mrs. North had handed him.

We made polite conversation for five minutes or so, then North said to me, "Paul, show Mr. Murray that letter."

I handed the piece of paper to Murray whose face registered astonishment as he read it through. "This is incredible," he said, "but it leaves me even more confused than before. If this cup is the Grail, then what was it doing in Rome?"

"I may have an answer to that," North replied, "but first let's have a look at the thing."

The tea tray was cleared away from the low table around which we were sitting, and Murray placed the vessel upon it, having removed the object from the wooden box. It was exactly as Dr. Tillit's letter had described: a cup with a wide, shallow bowl, perhaps seven or eight inches across, with a remarkable blue glaze on the inner surface, dark in the centre and fading toward the edges. North picked it up and looked at it carefully, then put it back on the table.

"I am convinced," he said, "that the series of events which brought this object here were not coincidences. Whether or not it is the Grail I can't yet be sure, but what I am sure is that it has some important role to fulfill or some important message to tell us. Diana is more psychic than I in matters of this kind, and I am going to ask her to see if she can read anything from the cup."

Mrs. North leaned forward and placed her hands around the bowl of the vessel. Then she closed her eyes and remained deep in concentration for a full ten minutes. After that time she leaned back and drew a deep breath. "No," she said, shaking her head. "It tells me nothing."

"Never mind," said North. "It will choose its own time to tell us what it has to. Meanwhile let me tell you my theory of how the cup might have made its way to Rome."

He walked over to the bookcase and came back carrying an old leather-bound volume. "This," he explained, sitting down with the book on his knee, "is an 18th-century book on Glastonbury, and it gives a detailed account of the events surrounding the dissolution of the abbey. The account includes an inventory of valuable objects belonging to the abbey that were sent abroad by the monks when they foresaw the dissolution." He turned the pages until he found the one he was looking for. "Here we are," he said. "Among the objects listed is something described as 'the Sapphire of Glastonbury'. And it goes on: 'This, the greatest of all the Abbey's treasures, was taken to Rome that one of the most precious relics in Christendom should escape profanation.'"

North closed the book and went on: "Now it does not say exactly what the 'Sapphire' was, but I am convinced that it was not a jewel, but an object the colour of sapphire, and it would have to be something pretty important to be described as 'one of the most precious relics in Christendom'. I believe that it was this chalice, and that the monks believed it, rightly or wrongly, to be the Holy Grail itself..."

He stopped talking abruptly and turned to look at the chalice which had started to emit a low humming noise. For several seconds we sat gazing at the object, mesmerized by the strange sound. Then, as we watched, the blue surface of the inside of the bowl became cloudy, and ill-defined shapes began to swirl across it like clouds reflected in faintly rippling water. At the same time the surface began to glow slightly like a television screen. Slowly the clouds grew fainter and the shapes began to take on a clearer definition. It became apparent that we were looking into a room in which seven people were gathered, five of them sitting on the floor, one of them in a chair, and the seventh standing.

Only these last two could be clearly seen. The person in the chair was a little, balding, wizened man with a toothbrush moustache. The man standing was gaunt and bony-faced with hair brushed forward over his forehead. He stood behind the chair and passed his hands in front of the other man's face and at the same time leaned forward and appeared to be whispering something into the man's ear.

At length the man in the chair seemed to lose consciousness, and his body went slack. The hypnotist stepped back and sat down on the floor with the others. Then the man in the chair stiffened again and his lips began to move. The man who had hypnotized him nodded occasionally as though he were listening to instructions. The speaker then began pointing to various members of the group who also nodded obediently. Finally the figure in the chair slumped again, and the hypnotist stepped forward and brought him out of his trance. After that the bowl went blurred, then cleared, and we were once more looking at the plain blue surface.

For a few seconds we remained silently staring at the place where the image had been. It was Rhys-Morgan who broke the silence. Leaning back, he said: "Well, if this thing is the Grail, that didn't seem to me very much like the Last Supper."

"No," said North in a quiet voice "what we saw was in a sense a hideous parody of a meeting between Christ and his disciples. It was a council of evil presided over by one of the princes of evil."

"You mean," I interrupted "that man in the chair was L.O.Q.?"

"No, the man in the chair was taken over by the mind of L.O.Q.

under hypnosis. L.O.Q. himself is rarely seen. He prefers to give his orders through a medium."

"But why," asked Murray, "should the Grail of all things – if it is that – give us such a vision?"

"Because it – or the power behind it – wanted to show us that L.O.Q. is up to something –something perhaps more evil than anything he has attempted before."

"Will it tell us any more, do you think?" I asked.

"I hope so," said North. "We must have another session after dinner. Unless we know exactly what L.O.Q. is up to we shall find it almost impossible to thwart him."

So later that evening the five of us gathered around the Grail again – for by then we were sure that it was the Grail. Once more we concentrated on the inside surface of the bowl. But this time no humming sound and no visions came. Try as we might we could not bring the slightest hint of a picture to the blue surface. After half an hour we gave up and agreed to try again the following morning. But on our next attempt the same thing happened, and when we tried again later the same day. After the third attempt we were forced to admit defeat.

"This puts us in a dilemma," said North, as we sat around the table gazing at the uncooperative chalice. "We have to find out what our friend L.O.Q. is up to, but it seems the Grail wants us to do it on our own."

We talked it over and decided that the only way to get the information we needed was for one of us to infiltrate L.O.Q.'s organisation and get as close to him as possible. North and his wife were out of the question for this task, as they were known to everyone in the occult world. Rhys-Morgan, even without his dog collar, had the air of a priest. And as for Murray, he was already well known as a writer and a man of Christian views. That left only me. There seemed no way out of it, so once again I found myself volunteering, rather unwillingly, for a dangerous task. But where was I to begin?

"I've been thinking about that," said North when I asked him. "I think I recognized the hypnotist that we saw among that group. I am not absolutely sure, but I believe he was Stanley Thompson. You may not recognize his real name, but he publicizes himself as a ritual magician under the name of Magister Zophas."

Now I remembered the man. He ran an occult order which was frequently the subject of sensational feature articles in the newspapers. I had seen pictures of the temple in his flat in Kentish Town where he initiated his disciples using some impressive regalia, candles, incense, and a hotch-potch of magical techniques. I had always assumed that his activities were innocuous, and it surprised me that he should be associated with L.O.Q. North, however, told me that he had long suspected something of the sort.

"Don't approach him with a direct request to join his order," North advised. "That might arouse his suspicions. Tell him that you are writing a book or article on the occult and that you would like his advice as a leading expert. Later you can pretend to become interested and ask to become one of his pupils. Get as close as you can to L.O.Q. without actually seeking full initiation into the inner order. If you did become a full initiate you might well find yourself in L.O.Q's power, in spite of my protection."

As I left the house, North and the others wished me luck, and I returned home wondering what I had let myself in for.

11

When I had arrived at the office on Monday morning I dialled the number that North had given me, wondering whether I should address Stanley Thompson by his real name or as Magister Zophas. In the end, when a female voice answered, I decided to use the former.

"Could I speak to Mr. Thompson please?"

"I'm afraid he's out," was the reply. "Would you like to leave a message? I'm his wife." Her voice was soft and pleasant, with a trace of Yorkshire accent.

I said that I was writing an article on occultism and would like to interview him. Mrs. Thompson said that she was sure he would help and that she would ask him to phone me back later.

By lunchtime he had still not phoned, so I went out to a pub with Simon. When I returned one of the tea girls, Maureen, came in and said that a strange man had telephoned. She was unable to remember his name, only that it was a "funny Indian sort of name." She said this with an expression of distaste. Anything foreign was anathema to Maureen.

"Was it," I asked, "Magister Zophas?"

"That's it. He said he'd be in this afternoon if you wanted to phone."

I picked up the telephone receiver and dialed the number. Almost immediately a rather slow, quiet voice with a Yorkshire accent said: "Hello, Zophas here."

When I gave my name he said: "Oh yes, I'm sorry I was out this morning. I was helping a would-be suicide."

I explained about the article I was writing and he offered to help in any way he could. We ended by arranging that he and his wife would meet me for lunch the following day at one o'clock at a restaurant in Covent Garden. He told me that he would be wearing a pentagram pendant around his neck.

I had chosen Singleton's as our rendez-vous on the spur of the moment, and as soon as I had put down the phone I began to have doubts about the choice. North would have been at home in its dim, Baroque, Edwardian elegance, but was it the right place to meet Stanley Thompson, alias Magister Zophas? This was the question in my mind as I waited there the following lunchtime at a table within sight of the door.

At five past one the door opened admitting a pretty, dark-haired girl of about thirty, then a man whom I recognized immediately as the hypnotist whom I had seen in the seance at Ravenhurst. He was of average height, but his thinness and his gaunt face somehow gave the impression of tallness. As I stood up and went forward to meet them I noticed the smell of some pungent and exotic perfume that emanated from one or both of them.

We introduced ourselves, and I gathered that Zophas's wife was called Moira. When we sat down my misgivings about my choice of restaurant became stronger. A group of men in business suits at the next table were giving us some very inquisitive looks. But Zophas seemed to be enjoying his incongruity. He lit up a cigarette with a flourish and then spent a long time scrutinizing the menu and commenting on the dishes before we ordered.

I said that it was very kind of him and his wife to come as I was sure they were very busy.

"On the contrary," he said, "Very nice of you to ask us. Besides, we haven't had much on lately, have we Moira?"

His wife shook her head. "No. The equinoxes are the worst times. There isn't a moment's rest then. The phone never stops ringing, and we're rushing about trying to get ready for the rituals. The equinoxes are the most powerful times for rituals, you see."

Zophas broke in: "Mr. Cairns probably understands about the equinoxes. I get the impression he knows something about this subject already." And he gave me a questioning, sidelong glance.

I shrugged. "A little. But I'd like to know more. That's really why I wanted to talk to you."

Zophas nodded. "Certainly, I can give you an idea of what magic is all about. But why not come to some of my classes? Would you like that?"

"Very much," I replied, pleased that such an opportunity had come so soon.

"Good. Our classes are on Wednesday evenings at eight o'clock. If you'd like to come along tomorrow you'd be very welcome."

So the following evening I found myself ringing the bell of a rather dilapidated early Victorian house in a quiet street off the Kentish Town Road. Moira answered the door and led me up three flights of stairs to the top flat. Half way up I caught the smell of incense wafting down. It was not the Indian kind, nor the kind that they burn in Catholic and High Anglican churches, but something subtly different – a sweet, heavy, pungent smell that I found rather oppressive.

The smell somehow matched the decor of the flat into which I was ushered. The walls of the dimly lit corridor were painted with a kind of *trompe l'oeil* design of Egyptian pillars, arches, and figures of animal-headed gods against a black background. One of the doors led off into a large living-room, which obviously doubled up as a temple. In one corner was an altar draped with red velvet cloth on which were placed candles, an incense burner and several statues of Indian and Egyptian deities. Other candles were placed around the room, shedding a soft, flickering light over the assortment of objects that hung on the walls: swords, round shields with Celtic patterns on them, Kabbalistic and astrological diagrams, posters of Tarot designs. A bookcase along one wall contained an oddly incongruous mixture of literature; besides magical and oriental books there was a whole row of Barbara Cartland novels in paperback. The whole effect of the room was rather tinselly – like a hastily-assembled film set.

"Make yourself at home. The others will be here soon," said Moira and left me alone in the room. I sat down on a sofa, and before long the members of the class began to arrive. They were mostly young people, the girls rather brighter-looking than the men, most of whom looked as though they would run for their lives at the first glimpse of a demon. There were also a number of older men. One I recognized as the little wizened man who had been hypnotized. There was also a large, rather plump fellow with a loose-lipped, pale face. A funny little mangy terrier was scuttling about everywhere, occasionally letting out a high-pitched bark.

The group seated themselves on chairs and on the floor, and about twenty people had gathered by the time Zophas himself came in and took a chair in the corner opposite the altar. The light from a candle on a low table beside him shone upward accentuating the hollows of his face. Moira sat in a chair next to him, and the terrier leapt up into his lap. The class fell silent, and he began to read from some foolscap sheets in his hand.

The substance of his lecture consisted mostly of things that I had already learned from North. The subject was visualization: the skill of building up pictures in the imagination so strongly that they took on a reality of their own which could then be manipulated by the magician. I already knew that any magician had to master this skill before he could use magic for any purpose, good or ill; and many of the exercises he described I had already practised under North's direction. He began by describing simple exercises using still objects such as flowers and trees. Once these had been mastered, he said, one could then go on to animals and finally people.

All this he read out at a painfully slow pace, stopping after every few words so that his pupils could take it down verbatim. Most of them had note pads and were scribbling away furiously. Every now and then the little dog on Zophas's knee would make whining noises, and eventually he attempted to subdue it by feeding it half a bar of chocolate. The rest he ate himself in between sentences.

This went on for about three quarters of an hour. Then the class ended, and Zophas announced that they would be reassembling at the "usual place" for anyone who cared to come along. The "usual place" turned out to be a pub around the corner called the Regency Tavern where another hour was spent drinking and talking, much to the interest of the local clientele. When it was time for me to leave I told Zophas that I had been interested in the class and asked if I could attend regularly. He seemed pleased and agreed without hesitation.

So every Wednesday for the next six weeks I turned up faithfully at the flat in Kentish Town and joined the group afterward at the Regency Tavern. Much of what Zophas taught I knew already, but I pretended that I had only a smattering of previous knowledge and managed to give the impression that I was a fast and eager learner.

Finally, one evening when I had arrived earlier than any of the others, I managed to have a conversation with Zophas on his own. I had been wondering how I could broach the subject I wanted to talk about, but he solved the problem for me by asking how I thought I was progressing. I said that I thought I was learning a great deal, but that I was still not quite sure what it was all aiming at. Though I could not ask directly, the question I wanted to imply was: when were we going to learn something about the Satanic side of magic? For nothing that he had said or taught so far could be construed as being "black".

"What we are aiming at," he replied, "is what all magic aims at: to turn the magician into a more complete human being by the worship of eternal forces."

This was the standard reply that any respectable magician would have made. I began to wonder whether perhaps North had made a mistake about his connection with L.O.Q.

"But I don't want to worship," I objected. "I want to control. I want power."

He gave me a sidelong glance and remained silent for a while. Then he said quietly:

"Everybody wants power, but not many people are willing to make the necessary sacrifices to achieve that power. Are you willing to make them?"

"It depends on what they are."

"In the kind of magic that you are talking about there is no 'depends'. You are either willing or not."

"Very well then," I declared. "I am."

"All right," he said after a pause. "I can see that you are of a higher calibre than the others. Come here tomorrow evening at nine and we shall have another talk."

When I returned home that evening I telephoned North and told him of my progress. He was surprised that Zophas was willing to take me into his confidence so soon. "I doubt whether he will actually invite you to join his inner order yet," he said. "He probably just wants to test you to make sure that you have the makings of a member of the black fraternity. But the test could be difficult. It is harder for a good person to feign evil than vice versa, and the slightest slip could give you away. To make it easier for you I will give you an object which will emanate evil vibrations – not enough to harm you, but just enough to keep Zophas happy. It will also absorb any evil emanations that might otherwise have passed off on to you."

So the following evening I called at North's flat before going on to Kentish Town, and he handed me a small wooden doll, about four inches long and crudely carved, with a hideous beaked nose and a malevolently grimacing mouth. The head, he explained, was hollow, and inside were some hairs and nail-pairings from a murderer. The doll emanated from one of the more unsavoury cults of the Caribbean and was charged with evil influences, but as it had been made for a specific purpose it would not bring any harm to me.

With this object in my pocket I made my way to Zophas's flat, and by the time I reached there the thing was already beginning to have an unpleasant effect on me. It was nothing that I could pin down – just a general feeling, like the faint smell of some rotting substance, that seemed to guide my thoughts toward destructiveness and decay.

The front door was open so I walked straight up the stairs. Something made me pause before the door of Zophas's flat, and from within I heard his voice in the hall, speaking into the telephone.

"Yes," he was saying, "it's all arranged. Father Brocart will be arriving by air this evening. That will give us tomorrow to get ready. I'd like you to meet him when he arrives. If I were to go it would attract the attention of the press." The rest of the conversation was lost in the sound of somebody flushing the lavatory in the flat below. When it stopped Zophas hung up.

I waited for a short interval and then knocked. Zophas opened the door. He nodded and without a word led me straight into the living room where a group of six people were already gathered: Zophas's wife and five whom I had seen at the classes, two young men, two girls, and the little middle-aged man with the toothbrush moustache whose name was Albert Sutton. They were sitting in a circle, cross-legged on the floor, except for Sutton who was in an armchair. I was told to sit on the floor, facing him. Zophas then stood behind the chair and began to pass his hands lightly up and down in front of Sutton's face, murmuring into his ear words that I could not catch. Within a minute a glazed look came over Sutton's face. Then Zophas walked to a position behind me and facing the chair. Suddenly he raised his voice.

"Master," he said, "are you with us?"

Sutton stiffened slightly and then said in a voice totally different from his normal one:

"I am with you. Let the business of the meeting begin."

With a shock I realized that the voice was the one I had heard in the Vienna bookshop and somewhere before that as well. But where?

"We bring before you," Zophas went on, "a candidate for admission to the inner order. He is ready to be examined."

Sutton, or the being that had taken over Sutton, then spoke to me

174

for the first time. "Look at me!" he ordered. I looked and then suddenly the glaze disappeared from his eyes and they became piercing and alert. As they stared at me I saw that, like the voice, they were familiar to me, but, more than that, I saw that I was familiar to them. A terrible fear came to me that their owner might know not only who I was but the real reason why I was there. When he spoke again, however, he gave nothing away.

"Why do you seek admission to the inner order?" he asked.

"Because I want power," I replied.

"Power to do what?"

"Nothing. I want it for its own sake."

His eyes seemed to probe deeper, penetrating to the very centre of my mind, and in that centre I tried to place the image of the doll. I felt its evil emanations, and I saw a hint of satisfaction come into the eyes before me.

"Very well," said the voice. "I can see that you are sincere in your desire for power. But do you understand that the kind of power you are seeking comes only through total obedience to a greater power?"

"Yes," I replied.

"And do you understand the ultimate purpose of that greater power?"

I hesitated, and before I could answer he went on:

"The purpose is to hasten the universe to its inevitable destiny. All created things must one day be destroyed. All of us who serve the power of which I speak live only for destruction and the exhilaration that it brings."

He paused, and I wondered if I was expected to say something, but he went on:

"I know what you're thinking. You're thinking: what about the world and its pleasures? What about food, sex, art, literature, music? Must they be destroyed as well? The point is that these are only temporary things. We cling to them as we cling to a crutch when we are lame. But when we are no longer lame we throw away the crutch. The purpose of the crutch is to make its owner able to discard it – and the purpose of everything in the world is to enable the world to be discarded, destroyed, annihilated. Just as a lame person can take pleasure in perfecting the use of a crutch, so we can take pleasure in using the things of the world for our purpose, knowing that they will one day be cast into nothingness."

As I listened I felt two forces pulling at me. All that I had learned from North pulled me toward a pinpoint of light that glowed somewhere in my consciousness; the doll, the voice of the man in front of me and the presence of the others in the room all pulled me downward into a whirling vortex of destruction.

The voice spoke again: "To be accepted as a member of our inner order a candidate must prove himself able to carry out our work unflinchingly. You will now be given a small preliminary test, and if you pass it you will be accepted as a probationary member. Later you will be given some real tests for full membership." Then addressing Zophas, he commanded that the test be prepared.

In response to the order Zophas stood up and went to the door into an adjoining room. There was a groan, then the sound of a slight scuffle, and Zophas reappeared dragging by the arm a girl who was gagged and had her hands tied behind her back. With a shock I recognized her as Angela, a member of the regular classes. She was tall and rather untidy-looking, with a soft, pale face. Her timid brown eyes now wore the look of a cornered deer frozen with terror at the sight of a pack of hounds closing in. She whimpered as Zophas tied her to a chair at the edge of the circle.

"This young woman," the voice went on, "betrayed her trust as a member of this fraternity and released information that was used to our detriment by the press. She is of no further use to us."

A feeling of nausea and terror came over me at the thought of what he might require me to do. But he read my mind.

"No," he said, "we are not going to ask you to kill her. The mind and soul may be dross, but the body can be used as a vehicle for a more worthy inhabitant – an entity from the inner hierarchies who can help us in our purpose."

I began to see that the mind which spoke through Sutton's mouth was capable of even greater depths of perversity than I had imagined.

"There is a being," he went on, "known as Iachadiel who partakes of the nature of the Moon and whose character strives after destruction. This girl was born with Sun in Cancer and is therefore of lunar nature and a perfect subject for what we have in mind."

The girl was now writhing in her chair, groaning and making pitiful animal grunts of terror.

"She is working up fear," observed the voice as though he might have been talking of a kettle coming to the boil. "That is good. It is part of our method." In a conversational tone he went on: "I don't know if you've heard how Pavlov discovered brainwashing. It was during the Leningrad floods of 1924. One day the dogs in his laboratory were accidentally trapped by flood water and only saved from death at the last minute. The effect of this experience was to remove from their brains all traces of previous conditioning."

Angela was now groaning so loudly that he had to raise his voice. "In this state," he continued in the tone of a lecturer contending with an unruly audience "the mind is ready to be implanted with new patterns. Of course we knew about such things long before Pavlov stumbled on them, and long before secret police forces began to use them in their clumsy way. We know how to use the swept-clean mind so that it becomes something entirely different.

"As to method, most of the work has already been done. The girl's fear has placed her in a sufficiently receptive state. Now all we need to do is to invoke Iachadiel to enter and take possession of her. Brother Zophas will perform the invocation. You will act as a focus and a channel by holding the appropriate talisman over the girl's head."

I had been searching desperately in my mind for a way to save Angela without giving myself away and so letting North down. Now an idea came to me. Instead of channeling the spirit of Iachadiel down into the girl I might be able to divert it into the Voodoo doll in my pocket. I knew that evil things accumulate more evil as a damp wall builds up salt and so attracts more damp. There was a chance that it might work.

Zophas handed me the talisman, a silver disc engraved with a hexagram, an outstretched are with pointing finger and a number of Hebrew letters. I slipped it into my pocket for a second and touched the doll with it to establish contact. Then, at Zophas's bidding, I stood behind the girl and held it over her head.

Zophas stood in front and began a long rigmarole in some harsh-sounding language that I did not recognize. His tone was deferential, and at intervals he bowed down. As he spoke the atmosphere in the room seemed to take on an extra heaviness on top of the now stifling smoke of the incense burning in a brass vessel on the floor. A presence was hovering there, waiting, seeking a foothold. I concentrated as hard as I could on the doll, holding its image in my mind, and soon I sensed that something was being sucked into it, in what felt like a stream of cold, stale air moving down from the talisman and along my body into the pocket where the doll lay.

The invocation lasted about fifteen minutes. When Zophas had finished I saw that Angela had fainted, and the voice speaking from Sutton ordered her to be untied. "Her personality has been destroyed," he said. "In a moment Iachadiel will show his presence." We waited, then slowly Angela began to raise her head.

I knew that I had to act before they realized that something was wrong. I was hesitating when chance came to my aid. One of the three candles on the floor sputtered and went out. I moved forward and quickly stepped on the other two. As the light went out I saw a flash of comprehension in the eyes that were not Sutton's eyes. "Quick, Zophas, bar the door!" said the voice.

But I was too quick. I grabbed Angela, was out into the hall and running with her down the stairs before the others started to pursue. She moved awkwardly, as her hands were still tied behind her back, but there was no time to untie them. A large black woman and her three children emerged from the flat below and stared in amazement as the two of us clattered down the stairs. She moved further out to see what was happening, and as I started down the second flight I saw Zophas collide with her and the two of them collapse into a heap on the floor.

We ran out into the street and around into a neighboring street where I had parked my car. I pushed Angela inside, got into the driver's seat, and was swinging out into the Kentish Town road when Zophas and the others appeared at a corner, looking around for their quarry. They did not see us, but I took no chances and jumped a red light. As I drove northward my hands on the steering wheel were shaking. As soon as I was sure that we were not being pursued, I pulled up and untied Angela's hands.

Earlier in the evening North had told me that he would be returning to Ravenhurst that night, so it was there that I was heading. I was sure that Zophas and his master would launch an occult attack against us, and I knew that we should be safe at Ravenhurst.

Within three quarters of an hour we were through the northern suburbs and into the country. I was aware that L.O.Q. would have no difficulty in following our route psychically, and I expected some kind of attempt to stop us reaching Ravenhurst. As we drew nearer my fears began to lessen, and I had almost forgotten the danger when, on a stretch of road through a wooded common, my headlights caught the shape of a deer standing directly on our path. It was a stag, and as we came closer I saw that there were three does with it. I slowed down, expecting the animals to continue across the road, but instead they remained standing, and I was forced to a halt. I switched off the engine and sat quietly not wishing to excite the stag, for I knew that an angry stag could break a windscreen with its antlers. Then I noticed something odd about the creature. It was standing perfectly still and its eyes were fixed on me, glowing in the beam of the headlamps. But they were not the eyes of a stag. They shone with the evil intelligence of some malevolent entity.

Angela, who had been in a state of semi-consciousness until now, suddenly gripped my arm with fear. I too was afraid, and when the creature began to move toward us the fear became panic. I felt trapped by the malign force emanating from the eyes as they came steadily closer. Then I became aware of another evil force closer at hand. Of course! The Voodoo doll was still in my pocket and now contained the spirit of Iachadiel. The thought came to me that I might be able to use it again in the same way as I had before. I took the doll out of my pocket and, reaching out of the window with my right hand, tossed it on to the road in front of the stag. The animal stopped, and the baleful light went out of its eyes. Then I saw a kind of luminous wisp of grey mist emerge from its head and disappear into the doll. The creature swayed and staggered for a moment as though stunned. Then it seemed to recover and trotted quickly off into the woods followed by the females.

Ten minutes later we were drawing into the courtyard of Ravenhurst. It was half past twelve, and the house was dark and silent.

But when we rang the front doorbell we heard from far within the reassuring sound of North's labrador barking. A few minutes later North himself appeared at the door in a dressing-gown.

"Paul!" he said, as we stepped forward into the light of the hallway. We both must have looked shaken, for he saw immediately that something had gone wrong. I introduced him to Angela and started to recount what had happened, but he stopped me with a gesture of his hand. "You can tell me later," he said. "First you must both have something to revive you."

We followed him back into the house. As we came to the foot of the stairs Mrs. North came down, also in a dressing-gown. I began to apologize for waking them both up so late, but she too saw what we had been through. "Come into the kitchen," she said "and I'll make you some supper."

As soon as we entered the big kitchen with its Welsh dresser, rows of massive mahogany cupboards and tiled floor, I began to feel a powerful hunger. Mrs. North soon appeased it with a vast plate of bacon and eggs and some strong tea, which we consumed sitting round a large plain wooden table. When we had finished Mrs. North showed Angela to a bedroom, leaving Gilbert and myself to talk. We went into his study and sat in the old familiar place before the fire while I drank a glass of his brandy and related the events of the evening.

What seemed to concern him more than anything was the conversation that I had overheard Zophas having on the telephone when he had mentioned that a priest called Father Brocart would be arriving.

"Are you sure the name was Brocart?" he asked.

"Yes," I replied "absolutely sure. Have you heard of him?"

"I have indeed. He is one of the most evil men in France. Hadley lived in France for a time and knew Brocart. He is an adept of great ability, which makes him all the more dangerous now that he is serving the evil powers."

For the next half hour North told me Brocart's history. His full name was Pierre Emile Brocart and he was born at Bordeaux, the son of a doctor. He studied for the priesthood at the local seminary and later in Rome where he took a doctorate in theology. He then joined a missionary society and was sent out to Latin America. Later he left the society and came as an independent priest to Paris where he made a considerable name for himself as a theologian. His wit, culture, and ability as a conversationalist made him a popular guest in the fashionable houses of Paris, and he became a well-known figure in society. But soon strange rumors began to circulate about Father Brocart. It was whispered that in Latin America he had been initiated into some devil-worshipping cult, and there were stories of unpleasant ceremonies in which he had taken part. The Church authorities investigated the rumors, and Brocart's name was fully cleared. But the whispers continued, and Brocart was obliged to leave Paris and return to Bordeaux where he set up a small religious community. Here he had remained unmolested until now.

"That is the outward story," said North when he had recounted these facts. "The truth is that by the time he established himself in Paris he was already a full member of the Black Brotherhood, and he used his position in Paris society to recruit rich and influential people to his cause. The society that he runs in Bordeaux is a cover for his Satanist activities. He is a man of very high rank in the Black Brotherhood – possibly even equal to L.O.Q. himself."

"Why," I asked "has L.O.Q. asked him to come over here?"

"Because Brocart is one of the few men in Europe able to perform the Mass of Saint Sécaire, the most powerful ceremony in the whole armory of the Black Brotherhood. It must be performed by a fully ordained priest, and it makes use of such strong currents that only a man of enormous physical and mental resilience can carry it out. But if successful its results can be disastrous. There is some evidence that it was performed on the eve of the assassination at Sarajevo that sparked off the First World War. And it is almost certain that it was used later to bring Hitler to power. If it is properly performed some great world-wide calamity always follows."

I asked him how it was possible for a single ceremony to have such widespread results. He explained that the world was covered with a pattern of lines of force joining centres of power. There were two networks of lines, one light, the other dark. By setting up a vibration from one of the key centres of the dark network, one could start a reaction that would have terrible repercussions all over the world.

"The way to counteract it," he went on "is to perform an opposing ceremony of equal or greater power in one of the light centres. In this country the obvious place would be Glastonbury where two powerful centres, a light and a dark, lie side-by-side. The only ceremony that would stand a chance of counteracting the Mass of Saint Sécaire is the

Ritual of the Four Rays which depends on the use of the original four sacred objects of the Tarot and of the Arthurian legend: the cup, the sword, the pentacle, and the wand. It's lucky that we now have all four. Fergus has placed the Grail in my charge." He chewed thoughtfully at his pipe and stared into the fire, then said: "The stone where Dr. Tillit placed the Grail is clearly a power centre of great significance. That's where we shall make our stand against Brocart and his friends. We shall need four people for the ritual. I shall ask Fergus and Hugh. Luckily Fergus is still staying at the vicarage." He looked at his watch. "It's three o'clock in the morning. I'll telephone the vicarage straight away and we'll set off for Glastonbury as soon as we can. The equinox is not until tomorrow, but the enemy may try to delay us."

We went back down to his study and he called the Vicar. It took several minutes before he came sleepily to the phone. North explained the situation, and half an hour later Rhys-Morgan and Murray arrived at the house. Soon after that we were all sitting in North's Rolls-Royce heading west.

12

We had not gone far before we met our first obstruction. Crossing the common we came upon a large articulated lorry which had slewed around and completely blocked the road. We stopped and got out of the car. The lorry driver was still in his cabin, badly shaken and with a large cut on his forehead where he had hit the windscreen, shattering the glass. He was conscious enough to tell us that he had been driving along when suddenly he had seen someone standing in the road directly in front of him – a man dressed entirely in black, his face hidden by a hood. The driver had swerved sharply to avoid the man and hit a tree on the right-hand side of the road.

I looked around and suddenly recognized the stretch of road. It was where I had encountered the stag the night before.

"That explains it," said North when I told him. "That doll that you threw on to the road must have caused the accident. We must find it. But when you do be sure not to touch it."

North had equipped us with torches before we set out, and now we began searching along the road near where the lorry had swerved. Soon Rhys-Morgan gave a shout, and we went over to him. At his feet was the doll, leering hideously in the beam from his torch.

"Stand back," North ordered. He then approached the doll, and we saw him perform what seemed to be a version of the pentagram ritual that I had seen him carry out twice before. After invoking the angels of the four quarters he called upon the entities inhabiting the doll to leave it and return to their proper habitations. As he did so the doll emitted a sort of wail, and a stream of grey mist swept out of it and went whirling up into the sky. North then picked up the doll and, having given it a final shake, put it in his pocket. "It's quite harmless now," he explained. "I shall donate it to one of the folklore museums."

We helped the lorry driver to a nearby farmhouse where the farmer was already up feeing his chickens and he immediately offered to give the man breakfast and telephone for the necessary help. The lorry's engine had not been damaged, so we were able to move it enough to get the car past, and after nearly an hour's delay we were on our way again in the half light of dawn.

In those days there was no motorway to the west, and our most direct route lay across through Reading and Newbury to Marlborough, then on down through Devizes, Trowbridge, and Wells. By the time we reached Reading the morning traffic was heavy, and there was a bottleneck in the town which held us up for another hour. Then, just past Newbury we ran into another snag. The road we had intended to take was blocked far ahead by an accident, and only single-file traffic could get through. It was some time before we learned the cause of the delay, and when we did we were still far back in the queue.

I could see that North was becoming anxious. Suddenly he decided to turn back in the direction we had come. "We'll take a more southerly route," he explained "and go down through Amesbury and Mere. It's a toss-up whether it will save us any time, but that hold-up could last for another hour."

We passed Amesbury without further hitch, and it was mid-morning when we came into the long, bare stretch passed Stonehenge. There were a dozen or so sightseers milling about in the Henge, spoiling the impression of timelessness that the place gives in the early morning. Nevertheless, there was something reassuring about the sight of those great stones. I wished that I could have stopped and stood in the circle feeling the presence of the ancient people who had worshiped there.

But we swept on, not even stopping for lunch. We ate sandwiches in the car, North munching as he drove.

In the early afternoon we had two set-backs in a row: first a flat tire, so that we had to change the wheel; then, as we came into Mere, a broken fan belt which caused the engine to overheat and sent a cloud of steam whirling round the mascot on the bonnet. It was only a short distance to the nearest garage, and we were able to drive there and arrange for the belt to be replaced. They said it would take half an hour, so we went to a hotel across the road for tea, a quiet, old-fashioned place where we were served by a motherly waitress in a chintzy lounge which we had to ourselves.

After she had unloaded our tray and left us North confessed that he was worried. As he poured out the tea he explained that the hold-ups we had experienced were not accidental. Someone was working against us, trying to prevent us from getting to Glastonbury.

"Is there anything we can do to fight it?" asked Murray.

For answer North reached into his pocket and took out a small copper object which he held up for us to see. It was shaped like a cross except that the top arm was in the form of a loop. We leaned forward to examine it.

"This," he said "is an ankh, the ancient Egyptian symbol of life. It was used by the pharaohs as a protection against evil." I remembered seeing reliefs of Egyptian kings processing, with one arm stretched out in front holding the ankh as though to ward off some unseen enemy.

"It is particularly useful," North went on "for overcoming magical barriers erected by a negative force. But in order for it to be fully effective it must be visualized and held with the inner eye so that the mind becomes an ankh-like force thrusting forward through the barriers."

"But why not use the Grail?" said Rhys-Morgan, pointing to the Gladstone bag on the floor beside North which contained the three holy objects. "Surely that would be even more effective."

"We could use the Grail," North replied "or for that matter the sword or pentacle, but I would prefer to reserve them for the real fight which is to come. For the time being we shall use the ankh. I want all three of you to memorize the shape and keep it in your inner consciousness for the rest of the journey."

We did not have to wait long for our chance to test the powers of the ankh symbol. Having paid our bill at the hotel we picked up the car from the garage and set off again. Half way to Wincanton the traffic in front of us slowed down and then halted. A hundred yards or so ahead a large herd of cows had escaped on to the road through a broken gate. They seemed to be in a stubborn sort of mood, and several of them were standing motionless in a line across the road.

North held up the ankh and at his bidding we closed our eyes and visualized its form. I tried to hold the image constant, but immediately it began to play tricks with me. The loop of the cross became a head and the central arm an absurd kind of bow tie. Legs sprouted from the lower arm, and from the sides a pair of arms holding a stick with a lotus-shaped fan at the end. The fan waved to and fro above an indistinct shape which gradually crystallized into that of a cow – not one of the cosy, innocuous brown-and-white cows on the road ahead but a magnificent, golden-headed cow with a great shining silver disk resting between her soaring horns.

Beside me North was chanting in some weird, alien key – a chant full of sounds never intended to be made by the European palate. One word, "Hathor", he repeated at intervals.

Of course! Hathor, the cow-goddess, the being whose task it was to guide the soul of the departed king to heaven. The power of the deity was all the greater because its form was that of the humble cow and not the mighty lion or the soaring eagle. Mundane things charged with unearthly power had a special force. I thought of the simple flail that the pharaohs. Carried as one of their symbols of authority, and of the cat that the Egyptians so much revered.

But I was forgetting the all-important ankh. I tried again to visualize it, but now the image had vanished. I saw only a landscape of sand and pyramids. The sensation of sudden movement made me open my eyes. And now it was the green landscape of England that seemed suddenly unfamiliar. The line of cars was moving forward again. The brown-and-white cows no longer blocked the road but were standing obligingly along the fences at the sides. They watched us impassively as we gathered speed and swept away toward Wincanton. And the golden-headed cow had gone as well. But we had all seen it. Rhys-Morgan and Murray described it as well.

I looked at North. He was laughing that rapid, breathing laugh of his. "The ankh and goddess have carried the day," he said "or part of it." He explained that all animals respond to an archetype of their species. By invoking Hathor he had induced the cows to obey his will.

Outside the car the rich countryside of Somerset swept by. The autumn colours were just beginning, the deep green of the conifers mingling with the lighter green tinged with gold of the beeches and elms. It had been a good summer, and combine harvesters were at work in the fields. A kestrel hovered over the roadside waiting patiently for its prey.

We were now within twenty miles of Glastonbury, but our difficulties were not yet over. Between Wincanton and Castle Cary we were held up for three quarters of an hour by a police check. A woman had evidently been murdered in a layby the previous evening, and we were asked if we had been passing that way at the estimated time. We said no, and the police waved us through without further question. Then, on a minor road further on, we ran into a sudden thick fog which dispersed after a great deal of hard concentration on the ankh on our part.

The nearer we drew to Glastonbury the stronger grew my awareness of the force which was opposing us. It was now affecting me physically, making me feel heavy and lethargic as though I had taken a sleeping drug. North felt it too. "We are coming nearer to the enemy," he said. "It's clear now that they are somewhere in the vicinity of Glastonbury, as I suspected they might be."

With seven miles to go we met sudden disaster. We were rounding a bend when we met another car which had taken the turn too wide and was straddling the middle of the narrow road as it came toward us. North turned sharply to the left to avoid it, and we thudded into a ditch. The other car had vanished by the time we had stepped out to investigate the damage. There was no question of driving on. The car would need to be towed out of the ditch, and besides the exhaust pipe had become dislodged and was hanging loose. There was nothing for it but to walk.

Strangely enough we felt less vulnerable on foot than we did in the car, though the air was surprisingly cold. Luckily we had brought overcoats with us, and, carrying our luggage, we set off in the direction of the Tor which we could now see rising up above the flat Somerset fields. North was carrying the ubiquitous Gladstone bag. Though we still sensed the countervailing force we pressed on without further hindrance, following the road.

It was early evening by the time we reached Glastonbury and collapsed gratefully with glasses of whisky in the bar of the George and Pilgrim after booking rooms for the night. I wondered why North had relaxed his rule about alcohol, but seeing my inquisitive look as he drank, he explained that the effect of the spirit would have long since worn off by midnight which was when we would begin our ritual and our enemies would begin theirs. Meanwhile he recommended that we fortify ourselves with a good dinner.

Over the meal North was back in his relaxed mood and seemed to be enjoying the strange looks we were getting from people at other tables. Obviously they had marked us out as one of the groups of mystically-minded eccentrics who frequent Glastonbury. Many of the local inhabitants do not appreciate the mystique of the place they live in, and distrust those who seek it out.

"Glastonbury is a strange place," North reflected. "Along with

Iona and Lindisfarne it is one of the three most spiritually charged places in the British Isles. But it is as though the spiritual currents are too strong for the locals. They have to make themselves oblivious to them in order to stay sane. You see there are two kinds of force at work here. First there's the light force associated with the Archangel Michael who has always had a special association with the West Country. You see that by the number of churches dedicated to him all over Somerset, Devon, and Cornwall. Usually they are situated on hilltops, and there's a whole line of them running through here and on down to Saint Michael's Mount in Cornwall.

"But there's a dark force operating here as well. The dragon has never been killed by Michael, only kept down. But occasionally he rears up and devilish things happen. When Christianity came to Glastonbury they build a chapel to Saint Michael on top of the Tor to rid it of pagan associations. But the dragon wrecked the chapel and left only the tower standing as a phallic memorial to the old religion. You see those pagans understood something that the Christians failed to understand. They were worshippers of the Sun, but they understood that darkness has a place in the scheme of things as well. The Christians who superseded them thought they could worship only the light, so they brought in the Archangel Michael as a solar figure and showed him keeping the dragon in perpetual submission."

Rhys-Morgan was beginning to look worried by North's line of talk. "Are you suggesting," he broke in "that we should let the dragon loose?"

North shook his head. "No, Hugh, not let him loose, but give

193

him a bit more rope. Otherwise he will go on as he does now, lying dormant for a while and then bursting out uncontrollably. That's why terrible things have happened in Glastonbury – like the hanging of the last abbot on top of the Tor. Our opponents know that the dragon is ready for another such escapade. They are going to try and give him a push, and they have chosen Glastonbury as the most suitable place to do it. But I think we had better continue this discussion upstairs."

Our coffee had just been served, so we picked up the cups and carried them off, followed by several pairs of inquisitive eyes. We went up to North's bedroom. I sat on the bed, the vicar and Murray on chairs, while North paced up and down the room.

"Where will they perform their ritual?" I asked.

"Possibly on top of the Tor," North replied. "But they won't be there yet. They will undoubtedly have a base near here – some country house within half a mile or so belonging to their brotherhood." He looked at his watch. "It's now nine o'clock. They will probably be setting out within the hour. But it would do us no good to attack them directly. What we must do is to find the Grail stone and perform a counteracting ritual there."

He spread out an Ordnance Survey map on a table and then took out his pendulum which he swung in a circle as he held it over the map. He passed it slowly across the map until it began to swing back and forth. He then marked the line of the swing with a pencil and moved the pendulum along it until once again the circular movement changed to a straight swing. At the point where the two lines crossed he tapped the map with his finger. "This is the spot," he said. "Here, at the intersection of these two footpaths." The place he pointed to lay in open country about half a mile to the north of the Tor.

He looked at his watch again. "Time we were going, in case we have trouble reaching the place." He picked up the bag containing the Sword, the Grail, the Pentacle and the Wand, and handed me another in which was the equipment for the ritual.

The town was quiet as we came out of the hotel and made our way toward the country. When we left the lighted streets and entered a dark, narrow lane, we switched on our torches. Soon the beam of North's torch lit up a signpost indicating a footpath turning off the lane to the left. We turned into it and went into single file with North in the lead. The path took us along the edge of a field and through a small copse.

The smell of the countryside at night took me back to my schooldays, to going on "night operations" with the officers' training corps at summer camp. It is strange how the mind fixes on trivial memories in times of stress. I recalled how we had carried radio sets with us on those operations, and the alphabet we had used for spelling out messages flashed through my brain: "alpha, bravo, charlie, delta, echo, foxtrot..." Why could they not have thought of something more imaginative? The names of demons for instance: "Abramelin, Beelzebub..." Their names seemed to be echoed by the wind that came sweeping over the flat stretches of the Isle of Avalon, stirring the trees, forcing us to stoop against its blast.

It was the wind that made me aware for the first time since we had left the security of the hotel that an unseen force was again building up against us, shifting vast tentacles of power somewhere out n the windy darkness, ready to clasp us in its baneful embrace.

Now we were walking through fog, and at first it did not strike me that wind and fog do not go together. Then I realized that this was no ordinary fog. It was rather like the kind they use in cheaply made horror films, which has an unnaturally heavy look, clinging to the ground n crude white masses. This had something of the same quality. It was not dispersed by the wind, but instead seemed to do the wind's bidding, forming itself into stealthy, curling shapes that brushed against me probingly.

With a shock I realized that I could no longer see the beam from North's torch and that I must have strayed from the path. The ground beneath my feet became more bumpy, with big stones here and there. I swung the beam of my torch round and could see nothing to guide me except a stone wall on my left. With mounting panic I began to follow the line of the wall. I called out to the others, but the fog seemed to stifle the sound and no answer came.

The ground became more uneven still with big clumps of grass and soft patches in between that showed I was entering an area of marsh. I stumbled, and my left foot sank up to the ankle in a pool. At the same time I clutched at the wall for balance, dropping the torch and cutting my left wrist on a sharp stone. Luckily my right hand still held the bag. The pain of the cut cleared my head, and the thought came to me that I might be able to use the ankh symbol to fight the forces around me.

Standing still I traced the symbol in the air, visualizing it as hard as I could. At the same time I chanted the sounds that I had once heard North chant: "Ee-ay-oh..." The fog seemed abruptly to ebb away, and somewhere, faintly but not far distant, I heard North answering the chant. I walked in the direction fro which it came and soon saw the light of his torch. But beyond it was another kind of light, a soft, bluish glow that stood out in the shape of a pillar.

"I should have warned you," said North when I reached him, "that they would try to split us up. But that was their last chance. We've reached our destination." He pointed to the blue glow, and I saw that it was coming from a large upright stone a few yards away, one side partly concealed by a thorn tree..

As we came closer to the stone I sensed that we had entered a different force field, a kind of oasis of energy into which the powers outside could not penetrate, though we could still hear and feel them all around us. We were standing in what seemed like a small temple of blue light. A moon, three-quarters full, had emerged from the clouds, and by its lights we could see the outline of the tor to the south. But there was something strange about it. The tower of the ruined St. Michael's chapel was bathed in a kind of red halo which spread out on to the hillside. This glow seemed to pulsate as though emitted from some great organism.

North answered our thoughts. "They have chosen the top of the Tor as I thought they would and are building up the power for their ritual. We have no time to lose. We'll perform our ritual around the stone, with each of us at one of the four quarters."

Rhys-Morgan, the man of religion, was given the western quarter where water and the cup reign supreme. North handed him the Grail, and I could see how he drew strength from it as he took it in his hands. Murray, the man of hot emotion, took the fiery south and held the wand. I took the airy east and held the sword, the cutting blade of the intellect. North, in keeping with his name, chose the northern quarter and the pentacle of earth, but before taking up his position he traced an invisible circle, invoking the four elements to guard it.

We stood and waited for midnight, when we knew that the battle would begin. Outside the invisible walls of sanctuary the wind continued to snarl; and mingled with it, only half distinguishable, were other sounds – murmurs and growls like a pent-up angry mob.

Suddenly these noises subsided as though in obedience to some higher authority which had taken command. In the lull we heard North say: "It has begun. They have started their Mass."

A flash of light came from the direction of the Tor made me turn back, and the red glow had suddenly increased in intensity. A moment later came a blast of wind, more violent than before, and brining with it an intense feeling of cold. At the same moment I heard North begin to recite the words of his ritual:

"Lord of the Universe and Prince of Everlasting Life, Master of Light and Builder of Eternity, Thou, who hast placed us here as defenders of the Light, give us the strength to oppose the forces of Darkness. I hereby beseech thy servants, the guardians of the elements and the quarters to aid us in this task..."

His voice was muffled by the wind which was now blowing so violently from the east that I had difficulty in keeping steady. I staggered back until I was leaning against the stone. The wind clutched at me angrily, and I felt that if I left the safety of the stone I would be tossed high into the air. Looking around, I saw that my three companions were also struggling. Rhys-Morgan was crouching on the ground, holding the Grail close to his body.

I felt the wind fling something at my head, something alive that clutched at my hair. I reached up and my hand touched a small, wriggling, flapping thing, which I brushed away with an angry cry. A second later I saw the outline of a bat against the moonlit sky, then another and another until the air was thick with them. I swung the sword at them, but they kept coming at me, tearing at my hair and making little squeaking cries. It was like being in a bad gothic horror film, only it was real and worse than any terror I had ever experienced. Somehow I summoned up the willpower to stand fast. I remembered North had taught me that the archangel of the east was Raphael, so I called his name repeatedly, holding the sword high above my head and pointing upwards. The cloud of bats gradually thinned out until there were none left.

But the wind was still blowing fiercely. It changed direction and began to blow from the north so that Gilbert bore the brunt of it. It was whipping up stones, bits of earth, leaves and fallen twigs and flinging them against and him. I saw him stagger slightly and then regain his firm foothold, crouching forward, the pentacle held up in front of him.

Then the attack changed direction again. The wind blew from the west and grew intensely cold, flinging hail the size of peas against us. It was Rhys-Morgan who took the full force of the hailstones, but he rose to his feet and stood firm, holding the Grail against the blizzard, and after a few moments the hail ceased.

Then the temperature suddenly changed, and a blast of intense heat came from the south. My eyes began to water, and a feeling of unbearable thirst came over me. The sound of running water came to my ears, and then I noticed that only a few feet from the circle was a little stream. For a moment I had the impulse to drop the sword and throw myself down by the stream to drink. Murray, facing the full blast of the heat, must surely have had the same temptation. But he stood in an aggressive position, crouching forward with the wand thrust out in front of him. Soon the heat subsided, and I looked again at the place where the stream had been it had vanished.

The wind dropped, and once again I could hear North's voice clearly. Simultaneously I saw that the glow coming from the Tor had dimmed slightly. But a moment later it flared up again with renewed force, and the elements began to attack us again in the same sequence. And so it went on for what must have been several hours. Each of us in turn would be attacked and would ward off the assault. The red glow would flare up, diminish and then flare up again. Gradually, however, it began to appear that each time the glow was slightly dimmer and the attacks weaker. But still North intoned, and still we held to our positions. I had the feeling that the ritual we were performing and the one that our opponents were carrying out nearby were both part of some much greater ritual.

Finally the glow from the Tor died away altogether, and the half-light of dawn began to take its place. The wind had dropped, and in the stillness I realized that North had finished his ritual. I turned and saw that he and the others were still in the same positions. But something was different. At first it was only the sense of an extra presence. Then I saw him. Beyond the eastern edge of the circle I could see the edge of a grey robe and an outstretched arm. The others had turned and were looking at him as well.

I saw the outstretched arm drop, and a moment later the figure stepped out into full view. We saw before us a tall man dressed in a priestly robe with a hood which half hid a lean, aquiline face of Latin or Semitic cast and complexion. He raised his right hand with the thumb and little finger pressed together in some secret sign. North silently returned the sign. The grey-robed man smiled, then turned and walked away. At the edge of a grove he turned and raised his hand again in a farewell gesture, then he disappeared into the trees. Moments later the sun blazed forth in the east, and the whole Tor was bathed in golden light.

13

The way back to the George and Pilgrim in the early dawn seemed surprisingly quick and easy. What had seemed vast, menacing shapes the night before were now revealed as innocuous-looking bushes or boulders. The patch of marshy ground over which I had struggled for what had seemed an agonizingly long time was now seen to be only twenty yards or so in length. The air was sharp and fresh, the birds were beginning their dawn chorus, and there was a feeling of lightness in the atmosphere as though some great burden had been lifted.

Not until we reached the hotel did we realize how tired we were. As soon as we arrived we went straight to bed and slept through until mid morning. Then we consumed a vast breakfast, once again under the curious eyes of the other guests who by that time were having morning coffee.

"What do you suppose happened to the others?" I asked North.

"Our opponents, you mean? I should think they cleared off as quickly as they could once they realized they were beaten."

"Do you think they'll try again?"

"That remains to be seen, but I doubt if they will – at least not for some time."

After we had finished our meal North went off to find a garage that could salvage his car. He intended to stay in Glastonbury until it could be repaired. Rhys-Morgan, Murray and myself planned to get a bus into Castle Gary and then catch a train to London. We had an hour to spare before the bus left, and Rhys-Morgan and Murray wanted to spend it looking round the remains of the abbey. I decided to take a walk up the Tor, half hoping that I might find some evidence of what our enemies had been doing there the night before.

I took a winding lane that led up to the shallow-sloping side of the hill. Then I was at the top in a matter of ten minutes or so. Strange, I thought, the tricks of perspective that the landscape plays on you in this region. I surveyed the view. Nothing for miles to break the fat, flat, lush countryside except this bare eminence, with its wild, savage, mysterious history, and a few miles to the south west the Tor's miniature replica, Burrow Mump, also topped by a ruined chapel to Saint Michael. I was alone on the Tor except for a few cows which had wandered to the top in search of better grazing. I walked round the tower and passed beneath the effigy on the wall of Saint Michael weighing the souls of the dead. What did I expect to find? What would the place look like after the Mass of Saint Sécaire had been performed there? All I could see were the remains of a fire. Strewn around it were some empty beer cans, some chicken bones, a half-eaten hot dog and some cigarette ends. It was hard to imagine Brocart and his cohorts pausing in the middle of their mass to have a smoke and a swig of beer. Puzzled, I sat on the grass and gazed at the view for a few minutes, then I walked back down into the town to catch the bus. On the way back to London I dozed most of the way. I arrived home with a feeling that an episode in my life had come to an end. But as it turned out there was to be an unexpected sequel.

Three weeks later I found myself in the West Country again to write about the remains of a prehistoric henge monument that had been discovered at Mount Pleasant, in Dorset. On the way back I had to pass through Dorchester, and it suddenly occurred to me to call on Dr. Tillit, the man who had written to my magazine about the Grail and how he had brought it back from Italy. I remembered the address because it was such an unlikely-sounding one: Arthur's Tower, Apollo Road.

It was half past two when I reached the town. With any luck Dr. Tillit would just have finished his lunch and might be able to spare me a few minutes before his afternoon surgery. I stopped to ask a policeman where the road was. He looked puzzled. "Apollo Road," he repeated. "I'm afraid I've never heard of it. That doesn't mean there isn't one though. Best ask the postmaster down the road on the right. He'll be able to tell you."

I thanked him and went to the post office where a brisk little white-haired man was in attendance behind the counter. He was also puzzled when I asked him where Apollo Road was. He consulted a map and could find no sign of it. Then he consulted the telephone directory for Dr. Tillit's name. It was not listed. Nor did it appear in any of the directories over the past ten years. "Well," he concluded, "it appears that your Dr. Tillit either doesn't exist or made up a false address." I said that it was kind of him to have taken so much trouble, and left the post office feeling very confused.

Driving back home I turned the thing over in my mind. It was not unknown for people to write bogus letters to the magazine. But in this case it was hard to see the motive. Besides, the events described in the letter had been confirmed by other events. I myself had seen the Grail. No, for some reason Dr. Tillit must have made up the address. Perhaps it was a kind of code. Arthur's Tower, Apollo Road. It was an esoteric enough combination. The light of Apollonian wisdom carried forward and enshrined in the Arthurian tradition? And the Tower? I remembered the lecture at that meeting in the Bloomsbury hotel where the

Kabbalistic Tree of Life had been transformed into an edifice of Arthurian symbolism. Perhaps that was the Tower that he meant.

I decided that I must track down Dr. Tillit, so when I arrived back at my office the following day I telephoned the Medical Register. They assured me that no Dr. Obadiah Tillit had ever practised in this country, at least as far back as their records extended. I thanked them for looking and put down the receiver. Then I picked up yet again the original letter from Dr. Tillit. There was the name and address clearly typed at the top of the page. Then a thought struck me. Surely a medical practitioner would not type his name and address. He would have a printed letter head. I was beginning to think that Dr. Tillit was a figment of somebody's imagination. It occurred to me that Murray might have invented him in order to dramatize his own experiences with the Grail to establish its miraculous powers in the eyes of other people. It seemed out of character with Murray, but I could think of no other explanation.

I was unable to discuss it with North as he had gone on a trip to India for several weeks in order to collect material for a book on Hindu mysticism. There was no one else who I felt I could turn to in order to calm my growing feeling of unease. I had left Glastonbury believing that I had participated in a stupendous event. For a while my whole being had felt imbued with a new force, like the golden glow that had surrounded the Tor. Now the affair of the fictitious Dr. Tillit had introduced a subversive element of doubt into everything. Arthur's Tower was rapidly turning into the Lightning-Struck Tower of the sixteenth Tarot trump. The whole edifice of the Tetrad, the Brotherhood – in fact everything I had experienced since meeting North – seemed to be crumbling. I began to wonder whether the whole thing had been a great charade. But I could not reconcile that thought with my belief in North. He had become a guiding light for me. The thought of any deception on his part would shake my whole universe.

Again and again my mind kept returning to the question of L.O.Q.'s identity. I felt that so many times I had been near to discovering it. If only I could put my finger on it I might have the answer to the whole mystery. I thought of the eyes that I had seen staring at me out of another man's face, the voice that I had heard in the bookshop in Vienna. I played them over in my mind like a film, hoping that the memory would click into place. I also acquired the habit of scanning the faces in a crowded street, on a bus or in a cinema, not knowing even if I would recognize L.O.Q.'s face when I saw it.

Then something happened that jogged my memory. One day, coming back to the office from lunch I was walking down the Strand when I ran into John Wakefield, the chaplain of my old college. He explained that he had been to a theological conference at King's College and was now on his way back to Paddington to catch the Oxford train. He had a few minutes to spare so we went into a nearby pub for a drink. It was an old-fashioned pub with a red carpet, dark wooden panelling and ornate frosted glass. We seated ourselves at a corner table with our glasses of beer. Suddenly Wakefield gave a start and began to stand up. He was looking at a tall, grey-haired man who had just come in and walked up to the bar. I heard the man order a whisky in an educated voice. Wakefield abruptly changed his mind and sat down again.

"I made a mistake," he explained. "For a moment I thought that man at the bar was Dr. Hardwick."

I looked again at the man. Certainly the resemblance to the Master of Leicester College was quite striking: the same tall, strong build, the same confident bearing, the same broad forehead and squarish face. The man reminded me of someone else as well, though for the moment I could not say who. It continued to trouble me after I had said goodbye to Wakefield and returned to the office. It continued to trouble me on the way home and throughout the evening. There had been something about that man in the bar. It had something to do with the Master and with Wakefield and with something else...L.O.Q. perhaps. I woke up suddenly in the middle of the night with the answer. That was it. L.O.Q. was the Master of Leicester College. Now I could bring to mind clearly the voice I had heard and the eyes I had seen across the common room table in Oxford. I had heard the voice again at the door of the Vienna bookshop and again speaking through the hypnotized Sutton in the Kentish Town flat.

Then another thought struck me, a thought which sent a chill through my whole being. I remembered suddenly the conversation I had had with Dr. Hardwick before dinner that evening and the interest he had shown when I had told him about the talisman they had unearthed in the Franciscan church. Now the mystery of Tim Bassett's death was explained. Hardwick had realized that he must get hold of the talisman as quickly as possible and had sent the Golem to cause the car crash.

I remained awake for the rest of the night wondering what to do next. The question marks in my mind were multiplying all the time. If Dr. Tillit was bogus then perhaps L.O.Q. was as well. A don posing as a black adept as part of some masquerade. But then how was one to explain the car crash and the disappearance of the talisman? I telephoned North and told him how confused I was feeling.

"Odd about the doctor, he said, but no doubt there's a simple explanation. As for Hardwick – well, you could be right, but it seems unlikely. Other people have similar voices, and I think you're reading too much into the business with the car crash."

I wasn't satisfied and decided to go to Oxford and confront Hardwick. I was able to arrange the trip two days later. As my car was out of order I took the train and spent the journey wondering what sort of conversation I was going to have with Hardwick. When the towers of Oxford came into sight across the untidy straggle of suburbs near the railway I began to think of turning back. The whole thing was quite absurd. How could a distinguished academic like Hardwick be a "saint of evil"? Still, I could perhaps see him on some other pretext and hope that he might give away some clue.

Still wondering what my approach should be I climbed into a taxi, and watched the familiar route into the centre of the town pass by. As we waited at the lights at Carfax I idly watched the faces of people in the street – housewives from Cowley doing their afternoon shopping, a little group of tramps huddling together at the corner, undergraduates slouching along in twos and threes with books under their arms. Most of them wore what was then the standard uniform of the young radical: faded blue denim suit and worn-out suede shoes. In spite of the beards they wore their faces looked young and vulnerable. I remembered with a sudden poignancy my own university days – the naive eagerness with which we had toyed with ideas, political theories, our own emotions and self-images. I felt both regret and relief that I was no longer one of them.

I was jerked out of my reverie by the sight of a familiar face crossing at the lights in front of me. For a moment my mind must have been frozen with astonishment, for I could not put a name to it. Then it registered: Tim Bassett. The certainty that it was he conflicted for a few seconds with the knowledge that he was dead. I sat motionless. Then, just as the lights were changing I decided to go after him and make sure. I thrust some money into the taxi driver's hand and ran into the Cornmarket in pursuit. Half way down the street I caught up with him. He turned to look in a shop window. He was wearing a khaki safari jacket and brown corduroy trousers, the same outfit as when I had last seen him.

He turned and faced me as I came up, out of breath. For a moment neither of us said anything. Then he spoke.

"Hello, Paul. You took me by surprise. What brings you to Oxford?" Then, without waiting for a reply, he added: "You're rather out of breath."

"Yes, the fact is I've been chasing you." My words sounded fatuous. I could think of nothing to say next. Are you really Tim Bassett? The question was clearly superfluous, but others were heaping themselves up in my mind.

He came to my rescue by suggesting that we have coffee together, and when we were settled in a small café nearby I told him the whole story about the supposed fatal accident in which he had been involved. He listened with interest, but without surprise.

"Yes," he said, when I had finished. "I thought something of the sort was going on. The Master of Leicester College telephoned me on the evening of the day that you came to see me about the excavations. He told me that some friends of his were going to spin a cock and bull tale about my being dead as part of a sort of..."

"A sort of what?"

Tim stirred the froth on his coffee. Then he took a sip before going on. "I can't really explain. You'd be better to go and see Hardwick himself."

"I was intending to." I was conscious of a touch of irritation in my voice. Tim was hiding something from me, and clearly it made him ill at ease. We passed another five minutes together, both of us in an embarrassed state of mind. Then I said goodbye and walked over to Leicester College. It was about twelve o'clock. I guessed that I would catch the Master before he went to lunch. He occupied an elegant house in a small, grassy quadrangle. I pushed open the front door and entered the small room on the left where his secretary – an efficient-looking white-haired woman – sat typing.

"Is the Master expecting you?" she asked.

I said no.

"Well, wait here please, I'll ask if he can see you."

She disappeared and came back a few seconds later to say that I could go in. I knew the way to his study. I had often been to sherry parties there as an undergraduate. I stood in the darkness of the hallway and knocked on the door. "Come in" said the voice with its now sinister familiarity.

I entered the study, a big room with two French windows looking on to a garden behind the house. The walls were lined with bookshelves and portraits in heavy gilt frames. The Master was sitting at a desk between the windows and sideways on to the wall. He half rose as I came in, and motioned me to a chair opposite him.

"How nice to see you, Cairns," he said warmly. "I think I know, by the way, why you have come."

As I still hesitated in front of his desk, he pointed to the chair again. "Please, do sit down." I obeyed, feeling that the initiative had somehow been taken from me.

"Would you like some sherry?" he asked. I said that I would, and he produced some glasses and a bottle from a glass-fronted cabinet behind him.

"There you are," he said, pushing a full glass across the desk toward me with the air of a chess player making a masterly move. "Yes," he went on, sipping at his own glass. "Gilbert North has told me – and I have told him – quite a lot about you."

He must have seen the look of astonishment on my face. "Yes, I have known Gilbert almost all my life. We were at school and university together. He has one of the most remarkable minds I have ever come across. He could have been Master of this college a hundred times over if he had wanted. He could have been a top public servant – anything in fact. Instead he went his own peculiar way. I used to think that he had wasted his talents. Now I know that in his own field he has achieved far more than I have done in mine."

The leaves of an old plane tree outside the window shook gently in the breeze, and a few of them drifted down on to the lawn of the little garden. A sprinkle of autumn sunlight fell into the room across the desk and the Persian carpet. I waited for the Master to go on, but he remained silent, contemplating his sherry glass.

"I am feeling rather confused," I began.

He laughed. "I know. Gilbert told me about that L.O.Q. business. Sorry to disappoint you. I'm afraid I'm not an evil adept, but I did have a part in the experiment." He took another sip from his glass. "It all seemed a bit theatrical to me when Gilbert suggested it, but then I suppose that was partly the point." He fell silent again.

"The point?" I repeated.

"Yes. I can understand your confusion, and I can't really give you a full explanation. Somebody else will have to do that. But let me just tell you this. Gilbert and I are both, in our own ways, concerned with the training of minds. Some time ago we found that occasionally a pupil would pass through my hands who was suitable for his – what shall we call it? – initiation. The combination of the two trainings produces a remarkable individual, of which Gilbert himself is the epitome. A contemporary of yours, Peter Rawson, was sent by me to Gilbert. You yourself were, as I sensed when you were an undergraduate, not yet ripe for his particular approach. But it did not surprise me when you found your way independently to his door. However, in your case something more than the usual training was involved. I don't think

I can go any further, but I will give you a letter of introduction to somebody who will spill the beans." He used the American expression with donnish emphasis as he might have done if he had been quoting a piece of Latin.

I watched him write out the letter and place it in an envelope. When he handed it to me I saw that the envelope was addressed to a Dr. Mario Bonetti of the "Institute for the Study of Non-Rational Motivation" in Keble Road. Hardwick rose from his chair with an air that suggested polite dismissal. Once again I found myself admiring his quiet authority. I shook his hand, thanked him for seeing me and, with the letter in my hand, left the college.

I had a sandwich and a glass of beer in a nearby pub, then made my way to Keble Road. The house I was looking for was part of a Victorian brick terrace, most of which was now occupied by university offices of one kind or another. I suppose that the Institute for the Study of Non-Rational Motivation was some kind of semi-private research group operating under the auspices of the university. I found the building and saw that the Institute's name was painted on a wooden board beside the entrance. I pushed open the door and found myself in a hallway with a linoleum floor. On the right was a doorway marked "Reception" behind which I could hear someone typing, rather slowly and haltingly, as though on two fingers. I entered, and a girl sitting at a desk with her back to the window stopped typing and looked up. She was very young-looking, perhaps seventeen or eighteen, and rather pretty, with a freckled face, turned-up nose, and red hair.

"Can I help you?" she asked, smiling.

"My name is Cairns," I said. "I've come to see Dr. Bonetti."

"I'm afraid he's not back from lunch yet. But he shouldn't be long. Do have a seat while you're waiting. I'll clear one for you."

She moved a pile of papers from a chair by the window. "Sorry it's so messy," she said. "I'm not really used to this kind of work. I'm only working here temporarily."

That explained the slow typing. The room was indeed rather untidy. There was a row of filing cabinets against the wall opposite the window covered with piles of papers – back numbers of journals, unfiled letters and the like. There were more piles of journals on a large table in the middle of the room, mostly on anthropology. In a rather nice Victorian fireplace a gas fire was going, making a gentle hissing noise. Over the mantelpiece was a framed reproduction of a Tibetan mandala – a series of gods and demons set in a pattern of concentric circles of different colours. The place had the curious atmosphere possessed by so many Oxford houses that have been converted for academic use – a not unpleasant mixture of the private and the institutional .I heard voices out in the hall, then a few moments later a youngish, dark-haired man in a brown corduroy jacket breezed in and began to rummage in one of the filing cabinets.

"Is Dr. Bonetti back, Frank?" the girl asked him.

He turned. "Yes, he's down in the basement talking to Carl. I'm just going down there. Shall I give him a message?"

"Yes, please. Could you tell him there's a Mr. Cairns here to see him?"

The man looked sharply at me when he heard my name. "Yes, certainly," he said, and left the room.

I waited, and a few minutes later the secretary's phone rang. "Yes," I heard her say, "I'll do that." Turning to me, she said: "Dr. Bonetti is free now. Could you go into his office? It's on the left at the end of the corridor."

I followed her directions, and as I entered the room a man was standing by the window with his back to me. When he turned I caught my breath. I knew I had seen him before, but the previous context had been so entirely different that for a moment I could not remember it.

He came forward and extended his hand. "How do you do, Mr. Cairns." This was the man I had seen dressed in a grey robe at Glastonbury. Now he was dressed in a pair of grey trousers and a tight-fitting black sweater, and he wore a pair of heavy, tortoiseshell-rimmed glasses.

I think he saw the recognition in my face, for he smiled slightly as he took the letter from Dr. Hardwick. He sat down behind a desk to read it, while I took a chair on the opposite side. On the pale blue wall behind him hung a row of little watercolours of landscapes, below which were some bookshelves filled mostly with volumes on psychology.

He nodded as he finished the letter and put it down on the desk. "Yes," he said, "I can understand that you must be wondering what has been going on." For the first time I noticed his slight Italian accent.

"I certainly am."

"That's understandable." He took off his glasses and leaned back. "Well let me try and explain. The fact is we owe you a sort of apology."

"When you say 'we'..."

"I mean my colleagues and I in this institute and also Mr. North. You see you have, without realizing it, been taking part in a kind of experiment, the validity of which demanded that the subject be unaware that he was participating."

"What sort of experiment?" I asked, a slight feeling of vexation beginning to mingle with bewilderment.

"I'm coming to that. We in this institute are concerned with exploring all types of irrational belief from a sociological and psychological point of view. One of the things which has struck us in our experience is how a very small number of irrational premises could be built up into a vast edifice of belief and behaviour totally at variance with what is normally accepted. Have you ever read James Hogg's *Confessions of a Justified Sinner?*"

It so happened that I had. I regarded Hogg, the "Ettrick Shepherd", as one of Scotland's underrated writers. Once I had even made a detour to visit the place in the Ettrick Valley where he had lived.

"Yes," I replied. "I seem to remember that the story was about a man who believed himself to be one of the elect of God. Wringham was his name, wasn't it? Robert Wringham."

"That's right. Well, you remember how Wringham is befriended by a mysterious individual who later turns out to be the Devil, and how the Devil uses Wringham's belief that he is one of the elect in order to induce him to commit murder?"

I nodded. "It's a fascinating story, but a little far-fetched."

Bonetti shook his head. "I disagree. I believe that Hogg was a man of remarkable psychological insight, far ahead of his time in his understanding of the human mind. There were many Wringhams in Nazi Germany. You see Wringham started from the premise that once you were one of the elect then *ipso facto* everything you did must be God's will and therefore justified. From such simple premises many similar irrational and dangerous systems have been built which have led their followers to do things which to an outsider seem senseless and abhorrent."

"You want to get rid of irrational tendencies altogether?" I interrupted.

He shook his head. "We can hardly do that, but we can perhaps inoculate society against them. In order to do that we have to understand them better. We wish to know more about the process whereby a person can be led to a set of ideas and modes of behaviour that are totally at variance with common sense and commonly accepted knowledge. I'll give you another example. Before the war there was a craze, especially in Germany, for a curious cosmology in which the Earth is regarded as a hollow sphere. We are on the inside, convex surface, and what we think of as space is in fact a massive inner sphere like the yolk of an egg with the stars dotted all over it. This theory was for a time toyed with by the Nazis, and they even carried out an experiment in which a rocket was fired vertically to see if it would cross the inside of the sphere and land on the other side of the Earth. Perfectly logical once you have accepted the initial cosmology, but total lunacy to an outside observer."

He paused. Interest was beginning to drive away my vexation. "And where do I come in?" I asked.

"Well, in order to observe this process right from the beginning we had to have a subject who was intelligent and critical and yet capable of being implanted with alien ideas. We also had to find a suitable set of ideas to use. Now we have a number of people whom you might call "field-workers", people who are interested in our work and supply us with their observations on human behaviour. One of them is Gilbert North. He contacted me one day and said that he had an ideal subject, someone who had come to him with advice about a dream..."

"And you decided to make me the guinea pig?" Suddenly my annoyance had returned.

"If you insist on using the term, yes," he went on unperturbed. Mr. North told us all about you and your interest in the occult. This was the ideal framework within which to conduct our experiment. We planned a complicated strategy involving the help of many other people, Tim Bassett, Stanley Thompson, Dr. Hardwick – even I played a small part, as I think you have recognized. First, like Wringham, you were to be convinced that you were one of an elect band. Then gradually various ideas were to be introduced to you: the existence of powerful talismans, golems, evil magical adepts, and so on – the object being to induce you to carry out acts of ever-increasing irrationality."

I thought with growing embarrassment of the rituals I had participated in.

"But what about the things I saw and experienced?" I objected.

"The spider-like creature who attacked us, the bull, the Voodoo doll, the battle at Glastonbury ."

"You may find this difficult to believe," he said, "but the spider and the bull were pure imagination, hallucinations induced by fatigue and extreme tension. The same applies to the wisp of ectoplasm that you saw curl up from the doll and the elemental forces that attacked you at Glastonbury. The lights on top of the Tor were coincidental – some teenagers having a bonfire party."

"What about Hugo von Falkendorf?"

"He was real, and so were the manuscripts and stuff that Mr. North bought from him."

"The tramp who stole the book from me?"

"An actor."

"An the girl I rescued from Zophas?"

"An actress. You see, we wove reality and illusion together. We didn't expect you to be quite so cooperative, but Mr. North was very skillful in integrating the images you produced into the broad occult structure he was building up."

"Of course we knew that at any moment you might tumble to what was going on – but that also was part of the experiment, to see to what extent the mind would refuse to raise logical objections once a particular line of thought had been accepted. For instance, why should our evil adept, L.O.Q., have gone to the trouble of slipping a Golem into Tim Bassett's car? And why should Bassett have calmly driven up the Woodstock Road with such an apparition sitting beside him? Perhaps the Golem was invisible to Bassett. But why then did the lorry driver see him? No doubt these thoughts occurred to you, but you rejected them, because they interfered with the main premises that you had already firmly accepted. Ultimately we would in any case have revealed everything to you, if you hadn't for yourself discovered what was going on."

"And how far would have taken me?"

"To the point where you would have been willing to commit, shall we say, a serious crime. Then we would have...intervened." The pause before the last word was disquieting.

"What makes you so sure I would have gone that far?"

"We are not sure. In that sense the experiment is incomplete. But we shall have to carry out several more experiments of this kind anyway before we can begin to draw any general conclusions."

One more question occurred to me. "What about the Grail and the things we saw in it?"

Bonetti rubbed his chin pensively before replying. "Certain things have happened in this experiment that even I can't explain – such as the phenomena produced by what you call the Grail ... the things you saw in it. The same applies to what apparently happened in the Vienna bookshop. I shall have to reserve judgment on these things until I have looked into them further. What is uncanny is how they fitted into the scenario of the experiment."

I could think of nothing more to say. Suddenly I began to be rather appalled by this institute and its purposes.

The door opened and the red-haired receptionist came in with some letters. Dr. Bonetti looked at his watch and then said to the girl:

"I think it's about time we had some tea, Kate." He turned and asked me if I would like some.

"No thank you," I said, "I really must be going."

"Oh there's no need for you to rush off yet," said Bonetti. "I must show you round the Institute." I didn't like his imperative tone.

"No, I must go," I insisted. "I have a train to catch back to London." I now had a strong urge to escape from the place. I stood up and shook hands with Bonetti before he could object. The girl smiled at me as she held open the door. I wondered if she was to be the next "subject" or whether she might have been intended for some part in the charade.

I was relieved when I was out in the street again. I had in fact three quarters of an hour to spare until the train, but I still walked as fast as I could to the station.

14

A few days before my visit to Oxford I had been offered a job on a magazine in Los Angeles and had been debating in my mind whether or not to accept it. On the positive side was the prospect of a high salary and the excitement of working in America for a while. The negative factors were the difficulties of letting or selling the house, putting our belongings in store and uprooting Mark from his school. Also in my mind had been the thought that there might remain important work for me to do with North. Now I was thoroughly confused about everything that had happened to me in connection with North, and in my unconscious unwillingness to question it all squarely I was seized with the desire to take flight. The offer from L.A. now seemed like a heaven-sent opportunity, and I wrote to accept it.

My conscience told me that I ought not to go before seeing North again, but I kept putting off any attempt to contact him. One part of my mind told me that he had acted in perfectly good faith, and that I was wrong to feel aggrieved at the way I had been used in the experiment. But another part of me resented the deception that had been practised. A whole new world had been opened up before me and then revealed as mere illusion. It had been like seeing a magnificent film set for some Roman epic, with vast porticoes, marble columns, gigantic statues and sweeping flights of steps – but move your angle of vision slightly and you see the thinness of the walls, the *trompe l'oeil* painting and the scaffolding hidden at the back. I could not quite believe that North had carried out the charade merely in the interests of science. He must have had some other motive. I was curious to find out, yet clung to my resentment and my unwillingness to face what might be an embarrassing encounter.

Finally it was he who took the initiative. He telephoned me one day in November and suggested that we have lunch together at his club. He must have known what Dr. Bonetti had told me, but his voice gave no indication that he considered our relationship to have changed in any way.

The club turned out to be rather different from what I had

expected. It was housed in an unpretentious, plainly furnished but comfortable premises on the first floor of a building in Northumberland Avenue, with a bar, a sitting-room, a library and a dining-room. The place was crowded with a respectable selection of both sexes. I had somehow thought that North's club would be one of those male strongholds in Pall Mall or St. James's Street.

North was in the sitting-room reading a copy of *The Times* when I arrived. As we were both hungry we went straight into the dining room where the table next to ours was occupied by a group of three men and two women who, from their conversation, seemed to be from one of the ministries round the corner in Whitehall. Now I saw why North had chosen this place for our meeting. In these surroundings we could not talk openly about what he knew was on my mind. We should have to discuss more everyday things. I suspected him of using this delaying tactic to employ his powers as a conversationalist in order to put me in a less disgruntled frame of mind. And I was right. Throughout the meal he skillfully guided the conversation along his chosen lines, telling me about his travels in the Far East as a young man, regaling me with endless stories of encounters with Indian holy men, Chinese bandits, Tibetan monks. In spite of myself I found myself succumbing once again to his charm.

After lunch and coffee in the sitting room North suggested that we take a walk. As we came out into the street the thought came to me that he seemed even to have arranged the weather to suit his purpose. The sun had come out and it had turned into one of those clear, mild autumn days which seem to suit London so well, making one notice things with greater sharpness, the flight of pigeons against a tempera-blue sky, the unexpected panoply of a flower stall, the redness of the buses hurtling down Whitehall.

We strolled down to Charing Cross and into the Embankment Gardens, past the bandstand where a brass band was playing selections from Johann Strauss. I was reminded suddenly of Vienna, of Helga Weiss and the little bookshop in the alleyway. Had North told the band to play this particular music? Was it another cleverly-arranged scenario in which I was to play a pre-arranged part? In my present mood it was beginning to look more like a joke than anything else. All the same, I shook off these suspicions with the thought that I could easily become paranoid if I went on thinking that way. I looked at North. He was strolling along, quietly puffing at his pipe. Once he stopped to admire some autumn roses in one of the flower beds. It was he who finally broke the silence.

"Well, I gather that Bonetti told you all about the experiment."

I nodded.

"Tell me something," he went on. "Did what he told you make you feel that everything you and I have done together was valueless? I shall not be offended if you say yes."

Now he had put me on the spot. It would be churlish of me, I felt, if I did say yes.

I laughed. "Well, no hard feelings, of course, but quite frankly I can't see what value it could have apart from its value for the experiment, and I am not really qualified to judge that."

"Come now, you must have felt annoyed surely when you found out."

"To begin with, yes, I'll admit that I was annoyed. I felt that I had been led to believe I had seen miracles, only to find it was all part of a masquerade."

"I see." North re-lit his pipe and tossed away the match. "And what if I were to tell you that the experiment and Dr. Bonetti's institute were in turn part of a larger masquerade?"

"I wouldn't know whether to believe you or not. My sense of truth and untruth has been rather shaken recently."

North chuckled. "Well that's actually a step forward. Look here, you say you believed yourself to have witnessed miracles. In fact what happened was that you looked for the miraculous and found reality. Now you must learn to look at reality and find the miraculous. Look at that rose. Is it any less miraculous than a talisman that can conjure up forces from the inner planes?" He stopped and bent forward to sniff the pale pink blossom.

"You see roses rather more often," I said.

"True, but that does not make it any less marvellous. People are constantly looking for the sensational when in fact it is staring them in the face. Houdini used to amaze people by freeing himself from padlocked chains and escaping from a coffin which had been submerged under water or beneath several feet of earth. They did not know that he was able to swallow and regurgitate the key to the padlock, nor that he had trained himself up to an extraordinary degree of physical fitness and dexterity so that he could carry out complicated and strenuous feats at lightning speed. If people had known his secrets they would have been intensely disappointed because they credited him with miraculous powers. But consider how miraculous was the reality: a human digestive system that can be made to regurgitate an object at will, a body that can be trained to such a degree of perfection, to say nothing of the powerful mind and will that drove the body to those feats – a mind and a will that everyone possesses in some degree if only they knew how to use them if only they could be set alight by the consciousness of the miraculous that is all around us."

We sat down on a bench, and North went on: "There is a fashion today for what one might call the 'reductionist' philosophy. Matter is 'nothing but' a collection of atoms moving according to certain fundamental laws; life is 'nothing but' a complex chemical process; love is 'nothing but' an illusion based on conditioning and physical need. Those who preach 'nothing but' philosophy imagine that they are being objective. In fact they are being subjective in a negative way. Total objectivity is impossible for anyone. Everyone, even the purest scientist working in the utmost isolation, has to decide in the depths of his being whether he is going to say 'yes' or 'no' to the universe or else to postpone the decision, which is another way of saying 'no'. At the moment it is the no's who rule the world. It is up to the yes's to try and keep a sense of the miraculous alive."

By implication he included me in the yes's, and I cannot deny that even as he spoke the things around me began to take on a deeper meaning: the pigeons pecking about on the grass, the noise of the traffic on the embankment, even the old tramp with an empty whisky bottle asleep on the bench opposite.

"Tell me," I said, "Was it true what you said a few minutes ago – about the institute and Dr. Bonetti being all part of a larger masquerade?"

He gave me a searching look. "What do you think?"

"I think you're an old trickster, Gilbert" I said with a laugh.

He laughed also. "You are right, but remember that the trickster and the magus are often two facets of the same person. Think of Hermes Trismegistos – one moment he's a divine philosopher and sage, the next he's a juggler in the market place. And the line between real magic and conjuring is very blurred. The spiritualists in their séances will sometimes begin with a few faked manifestations – knocks, flying objects, ectoplasm and so on – just to create the right atmosphere before the real phenomena start to appear. And conversely, sometimes during a stage conjuring act real magic will happen."

I thought about this for a moment then said: "All right, so what else have you got up your sleeve? What is the larger masquerade that you mentioned?"

"That depends on you." He puffed again at his pipe. "Everything that you have experienced in the so-called experiment has in fact been a test. You proved your courage during the re-living of your rite of passage with the Wild Folk and during the magical battles that we fought. You proved your moral sense in the episode with Stanley Thompson, alias Zophas. You proved your ability as a ritualist in our ceremonies. You proved your steadfastness in refusing to reject those experiences which you knew to be genuine when you found out that certain other experiences were faked. And you have proved your sense of humour during this conversation – a sense of humour is vital to keep one down to earth during occult work. You have passed the test well, and you are ready to play the great game ... now that the Tetrad is in place. You see, part of your role was to lead us to the Tetrad. Bonetti's experiment was the vehicle for bringing that about."

"And what is the great game?" I asked.

"You will find out soon. I am going to prepare a meeting with a number of other people to discuss certain important plans, and I want you to be there. I will contact you in a few days to give you the details and tell you where and when the meeting will take place. Meanwhile hold the next few weekends free."

It seemed the right moment to tell him about my forthcoming move to America. He frowned slightly and took a puff at his pipe.

"When do you leave?" he asked.

"Probably in a couple of months."

"I see. Then we shall still have time for the meeting before you go."

We walked up to the Strand, and he hailed a taxi. As it drove off he gave me a cheerful wave. It was the last time I saw him.

15

I never heard from North about the meeting, and in the preparations for our departure I forgot about it. We left for America at the beginning of the year, but our sojourn in Los Angeles turned out to be shorter than we had planned. We rented a house in one of the canyons of Santa Monica, and I drove into the city every day, working on the 20th floor of a brash new building in the downtown area. Almost as soon as I had arrived the place began to enervate and depress me. In Paris or Vienna or even parts of London the spirit can open out and breathe, but in Los Angeles one always seemed to be tearing along an endless freeway from one faceless suburb to another. It was true that the city had a certain atmosphere of thrusting energy that could for a short period be exciting, but it was an unnatural, feverish energy that left little room for genuine human contact. Though I encountered great warmth and friendliness among individuals I felt far more foreign and alien here than I had ever done in the countries of Europe. The job also turned out to be less interesting than I had hoped, and after nine months I decided to give it up and return to Britain. Sally had also found it difficult to adapt to the way of life there and was glad to come home. Only Mark was disappointed to be leaving as he had adapted quickly and made new friends. On our return we re-occupied our house, which we had let during our absence, and by a stroke of good fortune I was offered another and higher post on the *Townsman*. So the autumn found me more or less back in my old way of life.

I had written two letters to North from America, but he had not replied, and I assumed that he had been too busy. In the interval I had thought a great deal about what he had taught me, and I came to realize that it had changed me in a subtle way. Whereas before I had tended to sift through life looking for experiences that were rare and exotic I was now more inclined to pour myself into each moment as it came. I had ceased to regard it as important whether North's so-called experiment had been "real", and it was only out of idle curiosity that, after returning to England, I made enquiries at Oxford about the Institute for the Study of Non-Rational Motivation. I found that no such place now existed. Several times I telephoned Ravenhurst and North's London flat, but got no answer, so one clear autumn afternoon, rather like the one a year earlier when we had walked in the Embankment Gardens, I drove over to Ravenhurst.

I realized that something was wrong as soon as I entered the driveway. The grounds had a neglected look, in contrast to the house whose window-frames had been freshly painted in a harsh and unsuitable shade of blue. No dog came to greet me as I stepped out of the car, but as I approached the front door a stocky man in a check suit with dark, oiled hair, came out from a side entrance and asked me in a slightly patronizing voice if he could help me. When I asked for Mr. North he shook his head.

"No, mate, Mr. North doesn't live here now. This is Mr. Cuthbert's place. He took it over last month."

I looked blank, and he went on in an irritated tone: "You've heard of Mr. Cuthbert haven't you? Mr. Percy Cuthbert of Cuthbert

Properties." Now I remembered seeing the sign on building sites in London, and I began to have a clear idea of the sort of man Mr. Cuthbert was, a man who had made a fortune out of organized vandalism and now wanted to have a stately home as a badge of respectability. The man I was talking to would probably be called his majordomo or something similarly high-flown. I asked the man what had become of North.

"Dead and gone I believe," he said matter-of-factly. "Anything Mr. Cuthbert can do for you? He'll be back soon."

I said no. To meet Mr. Cuthbert was the last thing I wanted at the moment. As I drove away I avoided looking back. I wished I had never come.

Later I discovered that North had died unexpectedly of a heart attack and that his wife Diana had moved to a village in Berkshire where her elderly brother and sister-in-law lived. She had bought a cottage near to theirs. One day I received a letter from her saying that she would like to see me some time, and suggesting that I call in for lunch or tea if I happened to be passing that way. Soon afterwards I had to drive down to Newbury to visit an archaeological excavation for an article in the magazine, and I arranged to call on her during the afternoon.

She lived in a half-timbered cottage in the kind of old English village setting that American tourists enthuse about. There was a church, a green, and an old pub called the Red Lion. The cottage had its front hidden from the road by a tall hawthorn hedge. I walked up a brick path across the little front garden and knocked at the door.

When she came to the door I saw immediately that she had aged. Her face was thinner, the lines deeper, the hair much greyer. But in her dark eyes the strength of her character still showed through undiminished.

"Paul, how nice to see you," she greeted. Her vibrant voice had not changed either. "Come inside."

She led me through a narrow hallway into a wide living room with a low, beamed ceiling, a great inglenook fireplace and a window and glass door opening on to a garden.

I remarked what a nice house it was. Looking round I recognized many objects from Ravenhurst – prints and paintings on the walls, books in the crowded shelves, pieces of furniture.

"Yes," she said, "I've been very lucky really. Of course I was sad to have to sell Ravenhurst, but I'm afraid it was the only way. There was estate duty to pay, and I couldn't have managed the upkeep on my own. I had hoped one of my sons might have taken it over, but they have both have homes and families elsewhere and didn't want to take on the responsibility. So ..." She shrugged sadly. "I had to bow to the inevitable."

I guessed how difficult the past few months must have been for her – first her husband dying and then having to move out of her home. But already she had made a new home here, using her skill with interior decoration so that everything fitted in as though it belonged there.

"I put the kettle on when I saw your car outside," she went on. "Sit down while I get the tea together." She went away into a little kitchen built on to the back of the house and came back a few minutes later with a tray.

We sat down on the big, chintz-covered sofa that had been in the drawing room at Ravenhurst, and over tea and cakes she asked me many questions about my trip to American and my plans for the future. It was not until after she had cleared away the tray and I was preparing to leave that she mentioned the past.

"There's something that I must give you," she said. "Gilbert wanted you to have it." And from the drawer of a writing table she took out North's alchemical ring and handed it to me.

I held it in my hand, feeling its weight and a kind of warm glow emanating from it, as though North was reaching out to me through the ring.

"Are you sure?" I said. "I mean ... I feel honoured, but shouldn't it go to one of your sons?"

"No, Gilbert was quite emphatic that he wanted you to have it. Keep it and guard it well."

When it was time for me to leave she said: "When you met Gilbert for the last time, did he say something about a meeting that he was going to organize?"

"Yes, he wanted me to attend. He was going to let me know when it was to take place."

She nodded. "Well, I want the meeting to happen as he planned. I can't tell you more right now, but you will hear from me."

After we had said goodbye I went to my car and sat in the driving seat looking at the ring on my hand and wondering what Diana was planning.

16

For nearly a year I heard nothing more from Diana, and I was beginning to wonder whether she had dropped the idea of the meeting. Then came a letter from her. When I opened it I was astonished to see that the letterhead bore the address of Ravenhurst and the North crest: two black ravens on a green shield, surmounted by a red helmet. I was even more astonished when I read the letter:

"Dear Paul,

You will be surprised to see that I am back at Ravenhurst. I can hardly believe it myself. It's happened through a sort of miracle which I will tell you more about when meet, which I hope will be very soon.

You will remember that, when you came to visit me, I said that I was going to carry out Gilbert's plan for a special sort of meeting. Well, now it's going to happen – here at Ravenhurst – and your presence and that of Sally will be very crucial to its success, so I do hope you will both come. The planned date is the first Saturday in May, which I hope will suit you. If not, please give me some alternative dates. If that day is all right for you, then come at about five o'clock. We are likely to go on until quite late in the evening.

I won't tell you yet what the meeting is about except that it concerns what Gilbert used to call the 'Great Game'. All will be revealed on the day.

With warmest affection from your friend,
Diana North"

I wrote back immediately, saying we were both eager to come. We arranged a babysitter for the evening, but in the afternoon Sally developed a bad migraine headache and felt unable to leave the house. I offered to stay and look after her, but she insisted that I go to the meeting and said she knew it was important for me to be there. So I drove to Ravenhurst on my own.

It was a strange feeling, after I had inwardly said farewell to the place, to be turning into the driveway between the gateposts with the stone ravens, crossing the bridge over the stream and seeing the house come into view at the end of the avenue of chestnut trees. As I drew up in the forecourt another car drew up beside me and Dr. Bonetti stepped out and greeted me with a handshake.

"Hello," he said jovially. "I take it you've come for the meeting."

"Yes," I replied "but I'm surprised to see you here."

He laughed. "I'm wearing a different hat from when you last saw me."

"No experiment this time?"

He shook his head. "I should explain a few things to you before we go in. Let's take a walk in the garden." He led the way out of the forecourt on to a broad lawn fringed with herbaceous borders. "You see," he continued "I came to realise that my experiment was all part of Gilbert North's game. I was playing my part in it just as you were, and in the course of playing it I came to see the world differently."

"In what way?"

"I used to see myself as a crusader for rationality. The premise of our institute was that if you could understand non-rational motivation you could find ways to guard society against it. Hence our experiments like the one you were involved in. It was Gilbert North's idea, and I went along with it, even to the extent of playing a role myself, as you remember."

We were approaching the rose garden, and I remembered how I had once walked there with North.

"The trouble was," Bonetti went on "that things began to happen that I couldn't account for. You know, there's a shared lore among professional conjurers that occasionally real magic will happen during a performance – an extra rabbit appearing out of the hat, someone levitating without the invisible wire, a voice coming out of an empty box, a piece of equipment flying across the stage. Conjurers dread this happening because then they are no longer in full control of the performance. That's how I felt when I saw moving images appear in the chalice and when I watched you and the others doing your ritual at Glastonbury and saw the forces of the elements at work. I kept telling myself that North had set the whole thing up and that the things I was seeing were not real – and yet I knew that they *were* real in some other scenario that I didn't comprehend. That's why I'm here. I'm hoping that Diana will enlighten us as to what that scenario is. Shall we go into the house?"

"And what happened to your institute?" I asked as we walked back.

"I came to question its whole raison d'être. We were running out of funding anyway so we closed it down."

As we re-entered the forecourt we saw a taxi parked there. A man and a woman had just stepped out, and the driver was taking suitcases out of the boot. Evidently they were planning to stay the night. Coming closer, I recognised Helga Weiss and the old bookseller Wolfgang Kurz from Vienna. After they had both shaken hands with me and I had introduced them to Bonetti, the bookseller said:

"Well, we meet under less dramatic circumstances than last time."

I laughed. "You can say that again. What on earth happened after I left?" I was still wondering whether what I had seen in the Vienna vault had been real.

"It was a close thing," Kurz said. "I got away in the confusion."

"And those men?"

"The KGB agents? They were overcome by the fumes from the elixir and the things they saw. The elixir does that to people. Makes them see their worst nightmares. The agents must have fled from the building shortly after I did."

"And what happened to the shop?"

Kurz shook his head. "I had to move to another premises. There was some fire damage, and they needed the site to make a shaft for the new underground railway."

We all moved towards the open front door and saw that Diana North was standing in the entrance hall, flanked by two tall young men. She welcomed us warmly and introduced the two men as her sons, Philip and Randolph. The former had his mother's dark hair and eyes. The latter was fair and blue-eyed. Both had their father's long, aquiline face, and both were dressed in expensive looking tweeds.

While Philip took Helga and Wolfgang off to their rooms, Diana told us how she had been able to regain possession of the house.

"Just after Mr Cuthbert bought it," she explained "his business went bust, and he had enormous debts. He had to sell the house in a great hurry, so he put it up for auction. I had a bit of money put by, Philip and Randolph chipped in generously, and between us we were able to buy it back at less than the price we had sold it for. Luckily Cuthbert hadn't yet got round to modernising the interior, as had planned to do – perish the thought. Shall we go into the Hall?"

Seeing the Hall again in all its splendour gave me a deep thrill. Through a tall western window a shaft of late afternoon light flooded into the room, accentuating the shadows of the high, beamed roof and lighting up a portrait of Gilbert that hung over the massive stone fireplace in which a log fire glowed. The picture showed him sitting in an armchair, pipe in hand, wearing the amused, wry expression that I knew so well.

Tea things were laid out on the massive oak table in the middle of the room, and several more people were milling about, drinking tea and helping themselves to cakes and scones. The air was filled with a homely scent from the log fire. Dr. Hardwick, the Master of Leicester

College, was leaning casually against the mantlepiece talking to Stanley Thompson, alias Magister Zophas, while Thompson's wife Moira chatted to Tim Bassett and Angela, the girl I had "rescued" from the Kentish Town flat. Seated in armchairs close to the fireplace were the Rev. Hugh Rhys-Morgan and Fergus Murray. Across the room, peering at the contents of a large mahogany bookcase, was Hugo von Falkendorf.

As I stood there wondering who to talk to next, Diana came up steering a rather plump, elderly man, with neatly combed white hair and rimless glasses.

"Let me introduce Dr. Tillet," she said.

"Glad to meet you," he said in an American accent.

"Likewise," I tried to keep the surprise out of my voice. "It was you who wrote that letter to the *Townsman*, wasn't it? I tried to contact you when I was in Dorchester, but they told me at the Post Office that your road didn't exist."

He laughed. "You can hardly call it a road. It's only a couple of old cottages at the edge of the town. Our letters often don't get delivered."

"I couldn't find you in the phone book either."

"Ex-directory."

"But I made enquiries through the Medical Registry. I drew a blank there as well."

Tillit laughed again. "No wonder. I was registered as a doctor in America. Haven't practised since I retired to England. My wife is English, you see."

"And what you wrote in your letter ... about the cup, the Sapphire of Glastonbury – was it all true?"

"Absolutely!"

There was more I wanted to ask Dr Tillit, but I saw Rhys-Morgan waving me over to him and Murray. As I came up to them I could see that Murray was in a peevish mood.

"All I can say," he muttered "is Gilbert's led us on a fine caper! I've a guid mind to ask Diana to return the Grail to me." Catching sight of me, he said: "Ah, Paul, what do you make of it all?"

"Well," I said "I suppose we're all rather in the dark, but I'm hoping that Diana will explain things."

"Exactly!" Rhys-Morgan broke in. "That's what I keep telling him. Let's reserve judgement until we hear what she has to say. And you must admit, Fergus, Glastonbury was a damn good show if nothing else."

Fergus merely grunted.

Diana had taken up a position at one end of the room and was clapping her hands for attention.

"Please find a seat, everyone," she said. Then, when everyone was seated, she went on: "Thank you all so much for coming. If Gilbert were here ..." she looked towards the portrait "... as I believe he is in spirit, this gathering would gladden his heart." She paused, looking around the room. Everyone was now silent and watching her attentively. "All of you have played your different roles in a great drama of which Gilbert was the director, but the drama was only a preparation for something much bigger that he was planning. I believe you have all heard of the Order of the Sanctum Regnum, the Order of the Sacred Kingdom, of which Gilbert was a leading member until it collapsed just before the war. His dream was to revive the Order. I have called you here because the time has come to fulfil that dream." She paused and a murmur of surprise went through the room.

"Gilbert always felt," she went on "that the Order should be revived when the four sacred objects of the Tetrad were brought together again. This has now been accomplished. The Cup, the Sword, the Wand and the Talisman are safe here in the Temple. They are outward manifestations of four great principles in the universe and in ourselves. The Cup, the Grail, represents water, the womb, the gentler feelings and emotions, and also the perfection that our higher selves tell us we should constantly be seeking, even if we can never completely attain it. The Sword is for air, speech, communication and the sharp, cutting edge of the intellect. The Wand is fire, it is the sacred phallus, the force of passion and driving energy without which nothing worthwhile can ever be achieved. Finally the Talisman or Pentacle is the symbol for earth, for money and material resources, the bricks and mortar of life.

"Of course some of you may not believe that these objects are the original Tetrad, but let us treat them as if they were. This 'as if' is the principle on which all magic works. If we say "it is as if" with our full heart, soul and mind, then so it will be, and the Tetrad will become a source of light and inspiration, radiating out from our Temple here at Ravenhurst, on the soil of England, which itself is a Sanctum

Regnum, King Arthur's magical land of Logres, the Albion of William Blake. Its spirit still has much to give to the world.

"This is the Great Game that we are playing, to use Gilbert's term, and we are not ashamed to call it a game, because a game can change the world. Three and a half centuries ago another great game caught the imagination of Europe when a mysterious report was published in Germany – you may have heard of it – the *Fama Fraternitatis*, the *Fame of the Fraternity of the Rosy Cross*, better known as the Rosicrucian Order, said to have been founded in the Middle Ages by the legendary Christian Rosenkreuz. The report proclaimed a glorious vision – a synthesis of science, religion and the age-old wisdom traditions of alchemy and the Kabbalah, to be applied to the regeneration of humankind. The idea of the Rosicrucian Fraternity aroused a great wave of enthusiasm throughout Europe, yet probably no such Fraternity ever existed. The whole thing was a kind of game, the purpose of which was to plant a legend in the mind of Europe, the way one might plant a dandelion, so that the seeds get carried far and wide on the wind and take root wherever they land.

"Today we urgently need a similar vision. We need to re-unite science, religion and those ancient wisdom traditions so that scientists work in a spirit of reverence, as the alchemists did. We need doctors who treat the whole human being, not just the disease. We need educators who develop the soul and spirit as well as the mind. We need architects who understand divine principles of beauty and can apply them to our towns and cities so that once again we can be surrounded by beauty and harmony instead of by concrete wastelands. And, so that we don't take ourselves too seriously and fall into hubris, we need a spirit of playfulness. We need to be laughing sages, earnest jesters – in a word, players of the Great Game.

"In a few moments, if you all agree, we shall go down into the Temple and hold an inauguration ritual for the revived Order. Then we shall return here to the Great Hall for a banquet. And tomorrow I want each of you to go out into the world and plant a seed that will change the world in some way for the better, however infinitesimally. Periodically we shall meet here and tell each other of the seeds that we have planted." She paused again and scanned the room. "Now, are all of you willing to join with me in this Great Game?" Everyone was looking at her intently except for Murray who was frowning and looking at the floor. "What about you, Fergus?" Diana asked. "Are you willing?"

Murray was silent for a moment, then looked up and said slowly. "Aye, I'm willing, Diana. I confess I came here very confused, but ye've spoken well. I'll do my best for yer Great Game."

Diana smiled. "Bless you, Fergus. Then let us begin. We shall go first to a room where you will find tabards – the original tabards of the Sanctum Regnum, which Gilbert carefully preserved. Choose one that you like and put it on before entering the Temple. Now I shall lead the way."

As we moved towards the doorway leading to the cellar Stanley Thompson clapped me on the shoulder and said in his Yorkshire accent: "Well Paul, that was a fine escape you made with Angela. You played your part well."

"So it was all a test," I said "... all those sinister goings-on in your flat in Kentish Town."

"Yes, and you passed it."

There were others I wanted to talk to as well – Hardwick, Tim Bassett and Hugo von Falkendorf – but a moment later we were descending the stairs to the robing room. The doors of the cupboards were open revealing a rich array of tabards of the kind that heralds wear. They were in various colours and materials. I found one in blue, trimmed with yellow – a simple rectangle with an opening in the middle, so that you slipped it over your head and it hung down at the front and back.

When everyone was robed we processed down to the lower cellar and along the dimly lit stone corridor. At the end of it the door to the Temple stood open, and the Temple itself glowed in the light of many candles. I could see on the altar the four objects of the Tetrad: the Wand that the Gypsy woman had sold to me; the Talisman that Gilbert had kept locked away at Ravenhurst; the Sword that I had brought back from Vienna; and the Cup which had passed through so many hands before finding its way here.

Diana had taken up a position by the altar. She was dressed in a tabard of rich green, and on her head was a jewelled tiara that sparkled with a hundred different colours in the candlelight. She raised her arms upwards and outwards in the timeless posture of ecstatic worship and called out: "*Procul hinc abeste profani!*"

The Great Game had begun.

Afterword and Acknowledgements

This book was a long time in the making. I wrote the first version in the 1970s, more as a kind of meditation on certain themes that were preoccupying me at the time than with any thoughts of publication. It then essentially lay fallow for a couple of decades, unread except by a handful of friends, until I was prompted to offer it to my friend Vladislav Zadrobilek in Prague for his esoteric publishing firm Trigon. He accordingly had it translated into Czech as *Návrat Tetrády* and published it in a beautiful edition in 1998, although he felt that it could be improved. Some time later the English version was read by our mutual friend Michal Pober, a Czech who had grown up in England and then moved back to his native land after the fall of communism. I am most grateful to him for generously devoting much time and thought to making detailed suggestions for improving the story. Warmest thanks are also due to my wife Donate for her key input and to my long-standing friend Lionel Snell for his comments at a very early stage. I took their suggestions into account when doing a radical revision of the book in 2012, which included writing a completely new ending. When seeking a publisher, I asked the advice of Christina Oakley Harrington of Treadwell's Bookshop, London, who kindly pointed me in the direction of Mandrake of Oxford, run by Mogg Morgan, to whom I am enormously grateful for making the book available to English-speaking readers at last. I also owe a big thank-you to my friend

Leigh McCloskey, a visionary artist of genius as well as an actor and writer, for allowing me to use his image of the Magus from the set of Tarot trumps presented in his book *Tarot ReVisioned* (Malibu, California: Olandar Press, 2003). If ever there was an ideal cover picture, this is it.

Mandrake

Fiction

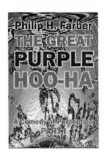

The Great Purple Hoo-Ha: a comedy of perception Part I
by Philip H Farber
ISBN 978-1-906958-16-9, £9.99, 232pp

Joe had a drinking problem. The possible demise of his
television talk show and the end of his career had tilted a very
big bottle of Old Mystery into his guts.

Now he was having trouble telling where the hallucinations
ended and reality began. Had the mysterious young man with the
cat – whom nobody else could see –really granted him a magical
wish for fame and fortune? Were the sex-obsessed cultists he was
investigating on the show really bringing on the End of the
World? Where did the sentient cream-filled pastries come from?
Who was the Most Disgusting Rock Star Ever? And, more
importantly, would Joe ever get his new girlfriend, the goddess,
into bed?

Part II
ISBN 978-1-906958-251, £9.99, 232pp

Joe climbed out of the hole into the gray light of a stormy afternoon.
Nothing was going as planned. He still hadn't gotten his girlfriend,
the goddess, into bed. The aliens never arrived and Elvis hadn't
returned. Up on the stage, robed magicians toting automatic weapons
called down unspeakable things from the sky. A crowd of a million
people was beginning to riot. And Joe knew that it was up to him,
the most famous man in the world, to save the day and bring forth
the Great Purple Hoo-Ha - if he could only figure out what the heck
it was.

As blatant propaganda, The Great Purple Hoo-Ha is funnier than
Catholicism and slightly less disgusting than ads for colonic irrigation.
-- Ivan Stang, Church of the Subgenius

Gateway to Hell By Margaret Bingley
ISBN 9781869928568 £9.99 paperback

A riveting black magic novel by popular author Margaret Bingley.
When their twins nephews are orphaned in a car accident, Nicola
and Howard offer the boys a home, unaware of the dark powers
they possess.

I, Crowley - Last Confession of the Beast 666 - *Almost* By Snoo Wilson
ISBN 978-1869928-544 £9.99/ $20 250pp
paperback

Aleister Crowley, otherwise known as the Beast 666, shared
membership of the Golden Dawn with W.B. Yeats, and publishers
with D.H. Lawrence. Now in a beyond-the-grave autobiogra-
phy, he recounts his own vocation, his practice of sex magic, and
his bruising encounters with his contemporaries.

Order direct from
Mandrake of Oxford
PO Box 250, Oxford, OX1 1AP (UK)
Phone: 01865 243671

Fax 01865 432929

Prices include economy postage

Visit our web site
online at - www.mandrake.uk.net
Email: mandrake@mandrake.uk.net

CPSIA information can be obtained at www.ICGtesting.com
Printed in the USA
LVOW052242130513

333477LV00002B/20/P